I am a good nurse, I love the children I care for, and that's all that matters.

She repeated the affirmation in her head, but it did little to divert her attention from the unsettling whole-body warmth she was experiencing in response to Richard's touch.

'Are you all right? Have something to drink.'

Clearing her throat, she tried to restore her self-control. But Richard's eyes were firmly fixed on hers, as if he had something important to say but was uncertain how to say it.

'I'm fine now.' She took a sip of the offered drink.

He put his carton of coffee down, ran long fingers through his mane of unruly hair and cleared his own throat. He finally spoke.

'I guess it's time to talk...about you and me.'

'Yes,' she whispered, and fixed her gaze firmly on the ground.

Dear Reader

The idea for this book was born after one of my writing friends had her head shaved to raise both awareness and money for a very good cause—the Leukaemia Foundation. That set me thinking about one of the worst things imaginable that can happen to a parent in their lifetime—the loss of a child to cancer. Fortunately more than eighty-five per cent of children diagnosed with cancer survive their illness and go on to lead full, healthy adult lives. So there is light at the end of what can initially be seen to be a very long, dark tunnel.

My hero is a paediatric oncologist and my heroine an oncology nurse. The people I know who work in this field are a truly dedicated group, who always have a smile or an encouraging word to give, no matter what the circumstances, and I hope my characters reflect those amazing qualities.

I make no apologies for planting Richard and Joanna in a very painful place at the beginning of their story. The challenge is for them to come to terms with (but never forget) the tragic events of their past, and find happiness in their enduring love for each other.

Of course the journey is not easy for them, but there are lots of joyful moments along the way—a scenario that mimics many real-life journeys.

I hope you enjoy the story of Richard and Joanna, and gain a little insight into an area of medicine that isn't always smooth sailing but that can be immensely satisfying.

Best wishes and happy reading

Leonie Knight

HOW TO SAVE A MARRIAGE IN A MILLION

BY
LEONIE KNIGHT

First published in Great Britain 2011
by Mills & Boon, an imprint of Harlequin (UK) Limited.
Harlequin (UK) Limited, Eton House, 18-24 Paradise Road,
Richmond, Surrey TW9 1SR

© Leonie Knight 2011

ISBN: 978 0 263 21923 4

Harlequin (UK) policy is to use papers that are natural, renewable and recyclable products and made from wood grown in sustainable forests. The logging and manufacturing process conform to the legal environmental regulations of the country of origin.

Printed and bound in Great Britain
by CPI Antony Rowe, Chippenham, Wiltshire

Originally a city girl, **Leonie Knight** grew up in Perth, Western Australia. Several years ago, with her husband, two young sons and their Golden Retriever, she moved south to a small rural acreage located midway between dazzling white beaches and the magnificent jarrah forest of the Darling Scarp. Now her boys have grown and left home, and the demands of her day-job have lessened, she finds she has more time to devote to the things she loves—gardening, walking, cycling, reading, and of course writing. The fact that she spent most of her adult life working in first a suburban and then a rural general medical practice, combined with the inspiration she gets from her real-life hero, makes it only natural that the stories she writes are medical romances.

This is Leonie's second book.
Why not check out her fantastic debut?

SUDDENLY SINGLE SOPHIE

Available from www.millsandboon.co.uk

I dedicate this book to all cancer patients, cancer survivors and their families. I also acknowledge the devoted and caring group of doctors and nurses who provide them with support, knowledge, hope and light through their journey towards the goal of recovery. They are truly an amazing group of people.

And to Claire, who had the courage and generosity to have her head shaved.

PROLOGUE

JOANNA cradled her tiny newborn son in her arms. Just three days old and so beautiful...

Although the journey she'd travelled in the past twelve months had not exactly been a smooth one, it had been worth every moment of the anguish and uncertainty. The perfect, fragile, sleeping child she held more than made up for the shock of finding out she was pregnant at the age of nineteen, when her chances of conceiving and carrying a baby to full term had been so low.

The living, breathing evidence of her love for Richard compensated a million times over for the blackness of her mind-numbing fear when she'd begun to haemorrhage at thirty-five weeks. She'd suffered the physical and emotional pain of the emergency Caesarean section without complaint because the result was akin to a miracle. After the birth she'd been told by her obstetrician that her chance of unassisted conception was even less than before her gorgeous little boy had arrived. That didn't worry Joanna. She had everything she had ever dreamed of snuggled up against her breast.

And Richard had been there for her all the way.

She was truly blessed.

Hearing the familiar sound of soft-soled shoes on polished vinyl, Joanna glanced towards the door of her hospital room. And she wasn't disappointed.

'Hello, you,' Richard said quietly before his gaze moved to settle on the baby…their baby.

'*Howell*, Samuel Benjamin. 2605 grams, 49cm. A precious son…'

The succinct words of the birth notice hardly did justice to the potpourri of emotions Joanna had felt—still felt—at bringing a new life into the world. It was a joy she thought she'd never experience.

Richard beamed, offering yet another extravagant bouquet of delicately scented yellow roses. He laid them, with the others, on the shelf above the compact desk. The room would be overflowing if she stayed in hospital much longer. He'd brought flowers every day since the birth and the tally now stood at three bountiful bunches.

She smiled. 'Hi,' was all she managed to say before her husband's lips covered hers and he delivered a kiss loaded with gentleness and joy. Sam's eyes opened briefly when his father ran a tentative finger gently across his little forehead. He then promptly drifted back into a peaceful sleep.

Taking a step back, Richard released a long, satisfied sigh.

'What was that for?' Joanna asked.

He hesitated a moment as if he needed the time to collect his thoughts. His voice was husky when he replied.

'You're beautiful. You've given me the gift of a perfect child and I think, at this moment, I must be the luckiest man on earth.'

He sat on the side of her bed and reached for her hand, covering it with his own before he added, 'And I love you, Joanna Howell… More than you can ever know.'

But she did know, had always known, and she knew that those simple words didn't do justice to the feelings they had for each other.

CHAPTER ONE

Eleven years later

It was Dr Richard Howell's first day at Lady Lawler Children's Hospital and a mix of excitement, anticipation and uncertainty churned in his stomach like cement in a fully loaded mixer.

It wasn't anything to do with the job, though.

The inevitability of bumping into Joanna again after spending three years working away in the U.K. had unsettled his nerves and filled his mind with memories, not all of them pleasant.

He snapped closed the latch of his briefcase at the conclusion of the interdisciplinary meeting which was held every second Monday morning in the paediatric oncology department. He still felt jet-lagged—he'd only arrived back in Western Australia three days ago—but was sure it wouldn't take long to get back into the swing of his hectic oncology consultancy.

'Coming for lunch?' James Francis, the paediatric surgeon, asked as they left the meeting room and headed for the lift. 'The food in the doctors' dining room isn't exactly gourmet but it's far superior to the canteen.'

'Not today.' Richard had seen a notice on the pin board of the ward reminding the staff of 'Shave or Colour for Kids'

Cancer Day'. Although he wasn't sponsoring anyone he'd planned to go down and watch, with the aim of giving the participants some encouragement and handing over a donation for a very worthy cause that was close to his heart. 'And I think I'll take the stairs. I need the exercise.'

'Suit yourself.' The surgeon's voice faded as the door of the lift closed. Richard bounded down several steps at a time and took a right turn at the bottom.

He remembered the canteen from when he'd worked at Lady Lawler on his paediatric rotation as a resident. That had been thirteen years ago, before he'd met Joanna and six months before he'd received his specialist training position at the Stirling, the largest children's hospital in the state. A year later he'd met and married Joanna and she'd presented him with a beautiful son the following year. He'd thought his life was as perfect as it could ever be…until their world had been ripped apart. They'd decided to separate and he had taken up a posting in the U.K. Two years had turned into three and he'd extended his stay for the simple reason that he couldn't face coming back—and seeing his wife again.

Yes, Joanna was still his wife, though they had been separated well past the official time necessary to apply for a divorce. Joanna had never pursued the matter, though, and he'd not had the desire or opportunity to remarry. So it hadn't seemed important.

But now he was ready to lay the demons of his past to rest by somehow making up for his cruel abandonment of his wife after the heart-breaking death of their son. He wasn't sure how he was going to do it and it had been a difficult decision to make. He was home and there was no turning back.

Richard glanced around the busy hall. There were a couple of familiar faces but no one he knew well enough to sit with. The canteen hadn't changed. Same monotonous menu of sandwiches, salad and a choice of a couple of hot dishes—

usually a lukewarm pasta and one of an endless number of variations of chicken and rice. He chose sandwiches and juice and then made his way to one of the few empty tables on the far side of the room.

The 'Shave and Colour' was well under way on a make-shift stage near the exit. Members of the nursing staff seemed to be the main participants.

His attention moved to one of the nurses who sat with her back to them, submitting to a complete head shave. What struck him were her incredible tresses. Her hair wasn't particularly long, but it was jet-black, thick and shiny.

This woman has guts, he thought. He couldn't think of a more powerful or personal way to show how much she cared for the children she was sacrificing a truly stunning head of hair for.

Who was she?

Richard had a sudden need to know. He wanted to meet her and tell her how impressed he was with her courage. He was intrigued, and interested in her motivation.

A few minutes later the woman on the stage turned around, grinning, her skull as smooth as a billiard ball. Her assured gaze flitted around the room as the canteen occupants clapped and cheered. She waved and smiled at people she obviously knew.

Then her eyes locked on his. The connection lasted only a few moments but it had a profound effect.

It was Joanna.

His wife.

He hardly recognised her.

She'd always had long hair, braided or swinging halfway down her back. Every time she'd gone to the hairdresser, she'd come home with different-coloured highlights and he couldn't believe he'd forgotten the magnificence of her natural hair colour.

And she'd gained weight. She wasn't plump but had healthy, rounded curves and colour in her cheeks. She also exuded a self-assurance he'd not seen in her during the eight years they'd been together.

Her appearance now reminded him of how much Sam's illness and tragic death had drained her. Now her trademark love of life had returned. He suspected she had managed to come to terms with the painful memories, as well as rid herself of any feelings she had for her estranged husband.

Her eyes were still fixed on his when her smile faded. It was if she was challenging him to pick fault with what she'd done...as if she knew he'd experienced a peculiar grief for her loss, both past and present.

The challenge was oddly exciting.

Richard's heart rate picked up a notch or two and he shook his head, trying to make sense of his jumbled thoughts. Probably jet-lag...hunger...first-day blues...

Part of what he experienced was raw, physical attraction and it took him totally by surprise. He hadn't felt like this since...

He looked away, unable to sustain contact with Joanna's unsettling gaze any longer. He attempted to finish his sandwich but it tasted like chalk and stuck in his throat as he tried to swallow.

Taking a deep breath, he decided he would go over and say hello. It wasn't as if his return would be a surprise to her. She knew he was coming back and that he would be working with her. He'd made enquiries and found out she'd added oncology nursing to her list of qualifications and that she worked on Matilda Ward here. So he needed to define the boundary between work and any remaining vestiges of their personal relationship.

As he stood Richard took his wallet out of his pocket and extracted a fifty-dollar note, but by the time he made his way over to the stage to make his donation, Joanna had disappeared, probably back to the ward and her patients. The combination of disappointment and relief left him heavy-hearted but he hoped he'd see her the following day when he officially started on the wards.

His thoughts were interrupted by his pager. He had an appointment with the hospital's medical director in ten minutes and he'd requested a reminder. He put the fifty dollars in the donation box.

It was time to file away his thoughts of the woman he'd once loved so fiercely and possessively and get back to work.

The previous week the nursing staff of Matilda Ward had had a detailed briefing about Richard Howell, the new head of the paediatric oncology unit at Lady Lawler, so Joanna had had plenty of time to prepare psychologically for his arrival. Lynne, the charge sister, had explained that, prior to a professional appointment in the U.K., he'd worked as a consultant at the Stirling Children's Hospital from the time he'd begun his specialist training about twelve years ago. Lynne understood that he was an excellent doctor and a pleasure to work with, she'd told them.

Once the practical details of his return had been discussed, the curious female staff had embarked on the predictable gossip session.

'How old is he?' one of the young nurses had asked. Their previous boss was retiring and was well into his sixties.

'Ooh, close to forty, I'd estimate,' Lynne had replied.

'Good-looking, I hope,' Karen, the play therapist who had just broken up with her boyfriend, had piped up.

Lynne had then scanned the group of inquisitive faces. 'I can't answer that one. I haven't had the pleasure of meeting him.'

'He'd have to be an improvement on old Dr Price. Is he married?' Karen had persisted.

Joanna had remained conspicuously silent during the discussion, but had felt the sudden heat of an unexpected blush at the mention of Richard's marital status. Fortunately the other women's attention had been focused firmly on Lynne, who had begun to put away the patient notes from handover. She hadn't quite finished her exposé on Dr Richard Howell, though, and the woman had glanced at Karen, who had never been shy of saying what she was thinking.

'Don't get any ideas, Karen. As far as I know, he's unattached. Separated or divorced, I heard.' She'd hesitated. 'Or at least he was when he left to go overseas.' She'd looked at the play therapist sternly. 'But I don't want your mind straying from the job. Which reminds me, that's what we all should be doing—working, not gossiping.'

Joanna had made a hurried exit and immersed herself in her work, trying not to think of the ramifications of Richard reappearing in her life. During the week before his arrival she'd tried to convince herself she would remain objective. Determined her relationship with Richard would be no different from her relationship with Dr Price, she'd devised an affirmation she'd repeated many times.

I am a good nurse, I love the children I care for and that's all that matters.

But when Joanna had scanned the room after having her head shaved and seen the tall, fair-haired man staring at her as if she had just committed a crime, her heart had done a back flip and *all that mattered* had been the connection she'd felt with a man she'd tried so hard to forget. She hadn't thought she'd see Richard until the following day when he officially commenced his clinical duties. She also thought she'd mentally prepared herself for all possible scenarios. Oh, how wrong she'd been.

Thank God she'd reverted back to her maiden name before she'd applied for the job at Lady Lawler. Even though Howell was a common name, she suspected there'd be the inevitable, light-hearted enquiries about whether she and Richard were related. She'd not told any of her colleagues the truth about her marriage and she had no plans to do so.

Seeing him again, after three and a half long years, had sent a surge of adrenaline coursing through her veins that felt like a slow-burning fuse. Her days of emotional fireworks were over, though. She'd worked hard to regain a meaningful life. She'd also realised there was no place in her future for a husband. She wouldn't run the risk of being abandoned again when the going got tough. Richard was her husband in name only. She'd put off discussing a divorce in the wild hope they might rediscover the love they had once shared in the early years of their marriage when Sam had been healthy and happy—the light of their lives. But Richard had not been able to cope with her grieving. He'd gone away and it was too late now.

I am a good nurse, I love the children I care for and that's all that matters.

The closer she came to a face-to-face meeting with Richard, the more difficult it became to convince herself, especially now his first day on the ward had finally arrived.

She opened her locker in the nurses' change rooms and replaced her casual clothes with the cheerful oncology staff uniform of coffee-coloured trousers and a crazy rainbow-patterned top. The outfit had been cleverly designed to have pockets in all the right places but bore no resemblance to the traditional dress of a nurse.

Thinking about the day ahead, she smiled as she stowed her gear in her locker. She wondered how Tye Coombs had coped with his final chemo the previous evening and whether Dylan's grandparents had arrived from the country in time to wish him a happy birthday. As she walked into Matilda Ward she was greeted by the usual bustle of the night sister gathering the day staff for the morning handover, but even their cheerful chat didn't distract her from thoughts of how she would cope with meeting Richard again. She tried her best not to appear preoccupied.

'My God, you're brave, Joanna,' Karen said as she breezed into the nursing station.

Joanna smiled. 'You mean my zero-gauge haircut?'

'Yeah, I didn't think you'd be game to do it again this year.' She ran her fingers through her own honey-brown locks, which still had the vestiges of purple glittered streaks. 'But then again, you can get away with it.' The woman studied Joanna's face for a few moments longer. 'I wish I had eyes like yours and that fine bone structure.'

Joanna laughed. 'I do it for the kids, and I don't think they notice the finer points of *bone structure*. I suspect you're just saying it to make me feel better.'

'No, I really mean it.'

The conversation was cut short by Lynne, the charge nurse for the day, summoning them all together.

'We've had a fairly quiet night and we actually have two empty beds, but I understand there's a thirteen-year-old boy coming in today for bone biopsy tomorrow,' Barbara, the night sister, began. 'And there was one new admission at about midnight. Cassie Blake's come in with a temp of 39.5 and a productive cough. Most of you know her, I think. Twelve-year-old with ALL.'

Lynne interrupted, 'Do you know what that stands for, Tracey?' She directed her question to the student nurse who had started on the ward the day before. The girl blushed.

'Acute…er…lymphoblastic leukaemia,' the girl amended.

'Well done. Sorry, Barb, go on.'

'No problem.' Barbara smiled and refocused her attention on the pile of patient folders. 'She's halfway through induction chemo as an outpatient and responding well. Chest X-ray's clear but she's on IV antibiotics and two-hourly obs. Temp's come down to 37.9 already. The physio will see her this morning and she's to have another blood count.'

Joanna became aware of the presence of a late arrival in the small nurses' station. By the hint of aftershave she knew the person was a male and he was standing directly behind her. She began to feel embarrassed that he had a full view of her recently shorn skull and as she moved sideways he leaned towards her and whispered, 'No need to move,' as casually as if he'd never met her before. 'I'm just eavesdropping.' Then he addressed the whole group.

'Don't let me interrupt, ladies...' he glanced apologetically at Grant, the only male nurse on for the shift '...and gentleman. Just thought I'd get a head start on the ward round by listening in. Hope you don't mind.'

'Of course not, Dr Howell.' Barbara beamed. 'I was just about to say that you would be seeing Cassie this morning to assess her.' She addressed the group again. 'You've all heard Dr Howell is starting his clinical duties today as medical oncologist, taking over from Dr Price.'

All eyes turned towards the man standing behind her. Joanna sensed the rush of warmth and felt certain her whole scalp was glowing. This kind of reaction was so out of character. She was embarrassing herself and behaving like a teenager.

'Thanks, Barbara, but please go on. Pretend I'm not here.'

Easier said than done, Joanna thought as she forced herself to concentrate on the remainder of the handover. It was no easy task with the man she had shared the most traumatic time of her life with standing so close she could feel his thigh touching her hip and the warmth of his breath on her neck.

She didn't want to draw attention to herself by moving again, though.

Barbara was finishing. Joanna cleared her throat but her voice still sounded husky.

'What's happened to Tye?'

Barbara laughed and Joanna thought she detected a hint of a wink. 'Even the prospect of his favourite nurse on duty today couldn't keep him here. He left last night, straight after his treatment finished.' She looked around the room. 'Anything else, any questions?'

There was an impatient silence. They were all ready to embark on another busy day's work.

'Great, I'm out of here, then. Have a good day.'

Richard's aim had been to get the feel of the staff attitude, the atmosphere of the ward and a rundown on the patients from the nursing point of view before his morning ward round. He'd had no idea whether Joanna would be working a morning shift so, when he saw her in all her close-clipped glory, he mentally rearranged his schedule.

She'd blushed at the mere sound of his voice; her breathing had quickened and he'd detected the slightest trembling of her hands when he'd accidentally touched her. He'd have to make an opportunity to speak to her alone, not only to reassure her that the last thing he wanted to do was to upset her but also to offer her an olive branch and let her know he wasn't about to intrude on the life she now had…unless she wanted him to.

He leafed through the case notes while Lynne allocated patients and duties to her staff for the day.

'Joanna will be coming with us, if that's okay with you, Dr Howell?' Lynne interrupted his train of thought. He didn't look up, but gathered the files and put them on the trolley.

'Fine by me.'

'She's the only nurse who gets to know *all* the kids on the ward and their families.' She chuckled. 'And a few of their secrets they won't share with anyone else.'

Now, why didn't that surprise him?

Joanna was again looking embarrassed, as if she wasn't comfortable with compliments—an unusual personality trait in an experienced, capable and obviously respected nurse. Richard dismissed the thought that his presence was the reason and focused his attention on what the charge sister was saying.

'We'll see Cassie, our most recent admission, shall we?' Lynne said as she guided them into the small room next to the two single rooms set aside for the special care of patients with severely compromised immune systems or serious infections that might be a threat to the fragile health of other sick patients on the ward. They all dutifully rubbed sanitising gel onto their hands.

'Cassie's been isolated as a precaution until we get confirmation of the nature of her infection. With your okay, Dr Howell, we'll move her into the general ward as soon as we can.'

Joanna entered the room first and Richard noticed the girl's face light up at the sight of her. Cassie's mother, though she looked as if she'd had little sleep the previous night, also managed a smile.

Joanna held up her hand in a high-five gesture.

'Love the new look, Jo,' the twelve-year-old said with a cheeky grin as their hands touched. Both mother and child were behaving as if Richard and Lynne weren't in the room. Their attention was entirely on Joanna…and they weren't the only ones. She had transformed on entering Cassie's room: she was now confident, charismatic even and seemed to have an aura of optimism hovering around her.

'Can't have you getting all the attention on the ward. I did it purely out of jealousy,' Joanna said.

Cassie smiled and then finally acknowledged that Joanna wasn't the only one who had entered the room.

'Who's that?' she said with the typical forthrightness of the young. 'Is he the new doctor?'

'Where are your manners, Cass?' her mother said as she stood to introduce herself. 'I'm Kerry.' She extended her hand.

'Dr Richard Howell. I've taken over from Dr Price and will be looking after Cassie for the rest of her treatment.' He turned to the girl and smiled. 'Hi, Cassie. I gather you're doing well with the chemo but you've had a setback. What's happened to bring you back to hospital?'

The girl looked at her mother then began to cough. It was a rasping, throaty cough and, combined with Cassie's good spirits, he doubted she had a serious infection.

'You tell him, Mum,' she said, slightly breathless from the exertion of coughing.

'Her brother had a cold last week. Cassie caught it, just a runny nose and a bit of a dry cough and I thought she was getting over it. She's in the middle of the cycle so I thought her neutrophils would be coming up and she'd be okay. But then last night—'

Cassie interrupted. 'I got a fever and started coughing some gunk.'

'And you know the rules about coming in—'

'If I feel sick and my temperature goes over 38 degrees. But it's come down, hasn't it, Jo? When can I go home?'

Richard looked at the chart. Her temperature had steadily and rapidly decreased since she'd commenced antibiotics and the last reading was just above normal.

Joanna looked at him for confirmation, with those huge brown eyes that he used to be able to read like a book. Not now, though. The window to her thoughts had the shutters jammed closed.

'You're right. It was close to normal when night staff checked an hour ago. It's all good news but I need to examine you.' He glanced at Kerry for approval and she nodded.

After checking Cassie's pulse, throat, ears and chest, the only thing he could find was a slightly inflamed throat, consistent with a viral infection.

'She's had a sputum and urine sent off?' he asked Lynne, but Joanna answered.

'And blood cultures. We should get microscopy back today but culture probably won't be until tomorrow.'

'Okay. Things are looking good, young lady, but we have to be sure we're giving you the right antibiotics. We'll get some results back today, including your blood count, but I'd like you to stay in until tomorrow when we'll have all the tests back and can be absolutely sure you're on the mend.'

Cassie frowned and her mother had a look of resignation as if she was expecting it. Neither spoke.

'I'll come and tell you the results as soon as they come through,' he added. 'And you can be moved to the main ward.'

'Thank you, Dr Howell.' It was Cassie's mother who spoke.

'Okay. And if you have any problems, I'm happy to see you and talk, answer any questions you might have.'

Lynne headed towards the door, a not-so-subtle indication she thought they'd spent long enough with their first patient, but Cassie had hold of Joanna's hand and was pulling her close. She made an attempt to whisper but it was obvious the girl wanted Richard to hear every word of what she was confiding to the nurse.

'You're right, Jo,' she said in a loud whisper. 'He *is* gorgeous, and much nicer than Dr Price.'

Richard couldn't help the tiniest smile that twitched on his lips.

Joanna had described him as gorgeous!

Certainly not a word he would use but it was the first glimmer of hope that the rock-hard shell she'd built to shield her emotions from him before they'd finally split up might have weakened with the passage of time.

'Sorry about that,' she said, averting her eyes and seeming to lose all composure. He couldn't work her out—confident and efficient one minute, quiet and uncertain the next. But he had little time to ponder her behaviour further.

'Where to now?' he asked, and dutifully followed Lynne as she introduced him to the rest of the patients and their relatives. Though it took nearly two hours to complete, he appreciated the sense of not being hurried, of being able to take the time needed to answer parents' questions and get to know the children, their problems and fears as well as their interests and pleasures.

And Joanna always seemed to know the right thing to say, to break the ice with a taciturn parent, persuade a retiring child to open up or a frightened teenager to express what they really felt. Richard was impressed. It was definitely two hours well spent.

When they'd finished seeing the last patient, a baby with an adrenal neuroblastoma recovering from surgery, Lynne excused herself, saying she had some administrative work to do before a teaching commitment with the student nurses.

'If you could take an early tea break, Joanna, can you take charge while I'm away?'

'No problem.' Joanna tidied the folders on the trolley. 'Is there anything else I can do for you, Dr Howell?' she said politely.

Yes, there was, and he decided to risk asking.

'Can I join you for your break, Sister Raven?'

Her eyebrows shot up at his use of her maiden name and the tormented look in her eyes asked why. The truth was he wanted to spend more time with her, alone, away from the distractions of the ward. He wanted to find out how she felt about him, but he certainly wasn't about to admit his motives.

'All right. I'll be ready in about five minutes.' Then she quickly walked away.

He stood watching till she was out of sight.

CHAPTER TWO

THE ward round with Richard had been an ordeal and Joanna knew she should have had more control. But she'd felt self-conscious. For no logical reason, she'd thought she had to prove she was a capable nurse; to show the man she had once been so dependent on that she'd managed to do something worthwhile with her life, something that didn't hinge on her being the perfect wife and mother.

On reflection she realised she'd been trying too hard. That realisation hadn't stopped her going into panic mode when he'd asked to accompany her on her break.

After the ward round finished she headed to the ladies' and glanced at the mirror. She looked no better or worse than usual but needed a moment to herself before going back. She took a couple of deep breaths.

A moment later, Tracey burst in and looked at her curiously.

'Are you all right? You look a bit flushed.'

'I'm fine. I worked a few extra hours yesterday and I feel tired, that's all.'

Without expecting a reply, Joanna left the restroom and hurried back to the main part of the ward, not wanting to keep Richard waiting. As she rounded the corner she saw him leaning up against the counter, all long legs, broad shoulders and sandy-coloured hair that seemed to have a mission to create its own style. He was deep in conversation with the pharmacist and looked up when she arrived.

'I won't be a minute,' he said with a friendly smile and then resumed his conversation.

How could he be so blasé when *her* emotions were in such turmoil?

She busied herself by checking through a bundle of test results that had recently arrived.

'Are you ready?' He stood looking over her shoulder and she could feel his warm breath on her neck. As she straightened up and turned he paused for a moment, dangerously close to her, eyes searching hers as if for the answer to an unspoken question, before he stepped back.

'You can finish what you're doing. I don't mind.'

'No, it can wait. I have to be back by ten because Lynne has—'

'A teaching session,' he interrupted with a smile. 'Where were you planning to go on your break?'

'To the canteen, if that's okay with you?'

The expression on his face changed. The relaxed cheerfulness and downright charm he'd spread through the ward by the bucketload that morning vanished in the time it took Joanna to replace the pile of reports in the 'in' basket.

'I was hoping for somewhere more private.' Richard loosened his tie and then cleared his throat, the only indication he wasn't as calm as he made out. 'You must realise we need to talk, and the sooner the better. If we're to work together...'

'Yes, of course.'

The space between them hung heavy with apprehension and she knew they had to reaffirm that the remnants of their marriage were unsalvageable. The debris of their broken relationship had to be tidily packaged and disposed of before they could comfortably move on and work together as part of the smooth-running oncology machine.

'The sooner the better,' she said quietly, and was glad Richard appeared not to hear.

He began to stride towards the doorway leading out of the ward and Joanna found herself battling to keep up with his pace. When he reached the door, he waited for her to go through first. It was a gentlemanly gesture that reminded her again of the man she used to know.

'Well? Have you any suggestions of where we could go without the company of half the hospital?' He kept walking towards the lifts and stopped when he arrived, pressing the button to go down. 'We could buy something to take away.'

Joanna suddenly had no appetite as thoughts scuttled through her mind.

Was it wise? To spend time alone with him?

She'd thought she'd never see him again. Her life had been uncomplicated, her future predictable. But now...

She didn't have time to think of an excuse to back down, though.

'What about the courtyard behind the clinics? It used to be so neglected...in fact, very few people knew it was there,' Richard suggested, and smiled for the first time since they'd left the ward. 'When I was an intern, about a hundred years ago, we used to call it *lovers' lair*.'

'Yes, it's still there.' Joanna looked away and somehow managed to suppress the bitterness that rose like burning acid in her throat. She'd been so young when she'd fallen in love with Richard. In her third and final year of nursing training, she'd naively thought she was a woman of the world.

He'd been her first and only lover, though, and she'd never wanted to know about his past. Of course he would have had girlfriends before he'd met her and probably had spent more time than she wanted to think about in *lovers' lair*. The fact that he was eight years older than her and had the kind of eye-catching good looks that stood the test of time… He'd probably also had lots of girlfriends since they'd split up.

The secret garden was what she preferred to call the hidden patch of jungle tucked behind the outpatient block.

Yes it was still there but *she* used it as a place of peaceful solace. She would often take advantage of the solitude the secluded area provided when she needed to compose herself, usually after one of her charges had died. Fortunately life, and remission from the terrible disease, was the more common outcome for children with cancer these days, though the word 'cure' was still used cautiously.

'What's the matter?'

Richard's words broke her reverie at the same time as the lift arrived.

'Nothing,' she lied. She wasn't about to reveal to Richard that everything about being alone with him was the matter.

A slight upward tilt of his eyebrows was the only indication he didn't believe her.

'Okay, let's get some food and then we can talk.'

The stilted conversation came to a standstill as they travelled to the ground floor but it didn't seem to bother her companion. When they arrived at the canteen, it was full to overflowing with orderlies and domestics, fortifying themselves for the working day ahead. There was also a scattering of nurses and every table was taken so Richard's suggestion to find somewhere else made good sense.

They bought cartons of iced coffee and, despite Joanna's insistence she wasn't hungry, Richard loaded up with snacks.

'I haven't had any breakfast,' Richard said as the woman behind the counter packed a large paper bag with his purchases.

'Your appetite's still as hearty as ever.' Joanna regretted the words as soon as she'd uttered them. Already she'd noticed so many things about Richard that hadn't changed—

the slight swagger of his hips when he slowed his usual brisk stride to a walking pace; the way his brow furrowed and the tip of his tongue protruded when he concentrated; the endearing dimple that appeared in his right cheek when he smiled, giving him the cutest lopsided expression.

But at least he didn't know how often he was in her mind.

He apparently read nothing more into her comment than a simple statement of fact.

'A bit too hearty at times. I've put on a couple of unwanted kilos during my stay overseas.' His tone was casual, as if he was discussing football scores with a mate. He didn't seem to expect a reply and continued, 'I need to get back into regular exercise.'

He paused as they arrived at the entrance to the canteen and waited for a group of chattering student nurses to come in then guided her out of the eating hall with a gentle hand on the small of her back. The simple gesture probably meant nothing to him. He'd always been free with those easy, tactile gestures that could set her heart racing.

He dropped his hand when they were through the doorway and set off at a slower pace she could keep up with.

'What was I talking about?' he said with a grin, and Joanna wondered if he'd been distracted by the group of giggling, nubile students who had cast blatantly flirty glances in his direction. A jolt of jealousy took her by surprise.

She had no hold on him, no right to be jealous, she reminded herself. They were about to discuss the best way to end a marriage that had floundered and failed dismally long ago, not have a friendly discussion about old times.

'Exercise,' she said in a voice barely above a whisper as they approached the clinic block.

'Exercise…that's right. I need to start swimming again, maybe join a gym. Do you know any decent ones around here that have a lap pool?'

She blushed, suddenly remembering all the weight *she'd* put on over the years since their separation. These days she never seemed to have any spare time for a disciplined fitness programme and her attempts at dieting had always been half-hearted; she liked food too much.

'Sorry, gym workouts aren't my thing.'

He hesitated. They'd arrived at their destination and it only lasted a few short moments but Joanna was acutely aware of her companion's head-to-toe appraisal. It was as though he'd stripped her completely bare.

'No, of course not,' he finally said with a smile. 'I imagine you get a decent workout with all the running around you do on the wards. Shall we go in?' He glanced at the entry to the garden.

Joanna's heart began to pound and her naked scalp prick-led as if each hair follicle had a direct connection with the emotions centre in her brain.

Why had she agreed to come?

But it was too late now to change her mind.

Joanna opened the vine-covered gate to the courtyard, which was indeed well hidden.

They sat on one of the bench seats in a corner. Richard handed her a drink and set the food between them, showing no indication he'd guessed how nervous she felt.

'Help yourself,' he said as he opened his carton of milk and took a long gulping drink. Joanna glanced at her watch. She definitely had no appetite.

'No, thanks.'

He raised one eyebrow as he peeled the paper casing off the muffin and popped a generous chunk into his mouth.

'Not on a diet, are you?' His eyes again wandered over her generously proportioned body but there was no sign of criticism in his tone. He had an unmistakeable twinkle in his eye, as if the statement was a challenge. Reminding herself she'd long ago stopped worrying about what people thought of how she looked, she refused to be unsettled by his question.

'Do you think I should be?' she said, rather more brusquely than she'd intended. She defiantly chose a Cellophane-wrapped portion of cheese and crackers from the selection of food, unwrapped it and began to eat.

'No, of course not. You're perfect just the way you are.'

Joanna nearly choked on an errant crumb. As she coughed to clear her throat, her eyes began watering and she felt a strong, warm hand first patting and then rubbing her back. It took all her self-control to stop herself from leaning into the blissful touch of his fingers on the exquisitely sensitive area between her shoulder blades.

She pulled away in alarm at the signals her body was sending. Fortunately Richard didn't seem to notice. His eyes were full of concern.

I am a good nurse, I love the children I care for and that's all that matters.

She repeated the affirmation in her head but it did little to divert her attention from the unsettling whole-body warmth she was experiencing in response to Richard's touch.

'Are you all right? Have something to drink.'

Clearing her throat, she tried to restore her self-control but Richard's eyes were firmly fixed on hers as if he had something important to say but was uncertain how to say it.

'I'm fine now.' She took a sip of the offered drink.

He put his carton of coffee down, ran long fingers through his mane of unruly hair and cleared his throat. He finally spoke.

'I guess it's time to talk…about you and me.'

'Yes,' she whispered, and fixed her gaze firmly on the ground.

* * *

'I saw you have your head shaved yesterday…' Richard hesitated. He was trying to break the ice by not launching into a discussion of their marriage as soon as they'd sat down. But the distressed look on Joanna's face left no doubt in his mind that he was being totally insensitive. She'd succumbed to a sacrifice most women wouldn't even consider, because of Sam. And probably because of every child with cancer that had been in her care.

'I'm sorry.'

Her eyes, which had been defiantly cast downward, found his and melted into a pool of heartache and exposed vulnerability. But it didn't last long. She slammed the door on her emotions and attempted a smile.

'What for?' Her expression was now as hard as steel.

'For…er…'

Why was it still so difficult to even mention the death of their son? He'd thought he'd regained some of his objectivity, but he should have realised that seeing Jo again would bring it all back.

She grasped his hand as if sensing his insecurity.

'We didn't come here to talk about Sam. He'll always have a special place in my heart and I'll never stop missing him but I can cope now. I'm no longer an emotional cripple and I've somehow managed to move on. It hasn't been easy but I've survived.'

From what he had initially thought of as Joanna's weakness had emerged a single-minded strength he envied. He was lost for words.

'We need to talk about our relationship,' she added.

She looked at him questioningly, expecting a reply.

'Yes.' Richard coughed to try and clear the stubborn lump in his throat but it refused to move. 'What do you want to do?'

He'd thought he'd worked through denial and regret and

could finally deal with seeing Joanna again…for closure. But he still had strong feelings for her and was suddenly over-whelmed by the thought that he wanted to save his marriage; he was reluctant to mention what had been his initial inten-tion—that they finally divorce.

It had seemed to be the logical solution to a problem that had been simmering in his mind ever since he'd made the decision to accept the position of head of the oncology de-partment at Lady Lawler. But now he'd seen Joanna again, it wasn't that simple. He needed to find out if she still had any feelings for him.

'Do you want—?'

'A divorce?'

Apparently easy for her to say and there was no avoiding the issue. But the goalposts had moved. He needed time. They were both older and, he hoped, wiser. When they'd married, Joanna had been nineteen and pregnant with a child she ex-pected she'd never have. The doctors had told her the scarring from a ruptured appendix three years previously had blocked her tubes and her only chance of bearing a child would be through microsurgery or IVF.

When she'd found out she was pregnant, they'd both been over the moon. Although they'd only known each other for a little over six months, they'd been insanely in love and the pregnancy had somehow validated that love. Maybe they'd jumped into marriage too quickly and for the wrong reasons. Many times he'd agonised over whether that was why their relationship hadn't been strong enough to survive the shat-tering stress of what had happened to their son.

Was it a bad thing to want to start over?

It had to be Jo's decision. She was the one who had suffered most and he didn't want to cause her any more heartache.

'Yes, I guess it comes down to that. We probably should have finalised things before I left for England, but—'

'I was an emotional vegetable and you couldn't bring yourself to add to my stress by going through a divorce.' She was actually smiling. 'I hated you for leaving me, you know. But I realise now that living with me at that time in our lives must have been a nightmare. Looking back, you certainly pulled out all the stops to try and bring me out of my depression. I don't blame you.' She sighed and then hesitated. 'I've moved on, Richard. I have a fulfilling life that doesn't involve a husband or children. Our marriage ended years ago and now it's time to formalise our separation.'

He cleared his throat but couldn't bring himself to say what he was thinking—he didn't deserve to be forgiven and it had been fanciful to even contemplate that she would give him another chance. Even if he hadn't gone away he had a feeling their paths would have diverged.

Why did he feel so gut-wrenchingly disappointed?

'I suppose so,' he finally said. 'Do you want me to get the wheels turning? I should have time to contact my lawyer some time in the next week.'

He couldn't go on. It all seemed so final, but Joanna was right. Why cling to the memory of something, no matter how beautiful, that could never be regained? They were different people from the young, naive nursing student and the indestructible, ambitious doctor who'd fallen in love more than a decade ago. Joanna had told him what he needed to know.

'That's fine by me. Let me know what I have to do.' She glanced at her watch, took a hurried sip of her drink and then stood up to leave. 'I have to go. I've got less than five minutes to get back to the ward and take over from Lynne.'

She paused a moment, as if waiting for his response, but looked anxious to leave. He needed a few moments to reprogramme his thoughts into work mode, though.

'Yes, of course you must go back. I have an appointment

with someone called Jodie to discuss accommodation, so I might see you later, back on the ward.'

She nodded, then leaned forward and kissed him lightly on the cheek, as if he was one of her charges to whom she'd had to impart particularly bad news.

At that moment he knew the thread he'd been clinging to in the hope they might get together again was finally broken. She'd stopped loving him long ago, and she was right. He needed to get on with his life. They both did. So why did it hurt so much?

CHAPTER THREE

RICHARD wasn't sure what Jodie Francis's job description was, but he was grateful she'd contacted him the previous day to enquire if he needed assistance to find accommodation. He'd forgotten about the block of half a dozen terraces tucked away two streets from the hospital and used as temporary lodgings for 'homeless' employees. In the past they'd been leased to visiting, top-level professionals who had temporary appointments such as post-graduate fellowships or academic posts. At the moment he was living in a holiday apartment, about half an hour's drive from Lady Lawler, and he hadn't thought far enough ahead to consider more permanent housing. He was eager to find out what Jodie had to offer.

He knocked on the door of a small office in the administration wing.

'Come in,' the owner of the youthful voice sang out.

By the time he'd opened the door she was out of her seat and headed in his direction with her hand extended in greeting.

'Hello, I'm Jodie, and you must be Dr Howell.'

The woman, who Richard estimated to be in her late twenties, grasped his hand and beamed.

'That's right. You phoned and left a message on the ward yesterday.'

He waited for her to sit down before settling in the austere, grey-upholstered chair opposite her desk.

She thumbed through a folder of papers and extracted a single page, which she placed on the top of the pile. 'I understand you've been back in Western Australia for less than a week and, er...' It was the first time the confident young lady had shown any sign of hesitation and Richard second-guessed what she was trying to say.

'You assumed, since I'd been away for so long, I might be looking for somewhere to stay?'

'Exactly.' She paused again. 'And am I right to assume... um...that you're on your own?'

'Yes.'

His heart rate quickened as a painful memory of a bleak conversation with his wife popped into his mind. When he and Jo had parted, he'd fully expected the break to be purely down-time to allow wounds to heal and that they would eventually reconcile. Their dream home, purchased midway through Joanna's pregnancy and lovingly renovated and decorated to accommodate the needs of their expanding family, had been a symbol of his wife's vision of their future together.

When Sam had died, that vision had been irreconcilably shattered.

Before he'd departed for the U.K. he'd assured Joanna the house was hers as long as she wanted it, but six months after he'd left she'd sent him a matter-of-fact email stating she wanted to sell the house and move into something smaller. 'More suited to a single woman' had been her exact words. But he'd suspected what she'd really wanted to say was *without the memories.*

It had broken his heart, and his phone call to her had done nothing to reassure him Jo had been coping any better than when he'd left. She'd stated calmly, when he'd offered to return to Australia, that it would be a waste of time and she didn't want to see him.

It would upset her too much, he read between the transparent lines of her conversation.

He had a sudden thought that he didn't even have her current address.

'You were saying?' the ebullient Jodie cut into his reverie, and he frowned, trying to remember the last thread of their conversation.

'Ah, yes. I'm separated and in the process of getting a divorce.' The words were out of his mouth, like a confession, before he had a chance to stop them. She'd not asked for any information on his marital status but he'd felt the need to explain why a thirty-nine-year-old consultant didn't have the wife and family that were often expected of someone of his age and position.

Jodie looked embarrassed and busied herself rearranging the papers on her desk.

'So what do you have to offer?'

The girl blushed crimson and Richard suddenly realised what he'd said.

'I didn't mean… I'm not…' he stumbled, and then they both laughed.

'I know.'

'Shall we start again?'

Twenty minutes later, Richard had signed a lease, organised for the rent to be deducted from his salary and taken possession of a set of keys to number 6B Peppermint Mews, the second house in the row of quaint terraces that the hospital owned. He'd made the decision without even viewing the place, on the basis that it was the only empty house in the row at the present time. The fact that it was fully furnished, he had a three-month lease with the option of staying longer and he could move in straight away added to its attraction.

There was a tiny light at the end of a very long dark tunnel, he thought as he said goodbye to Jodie and strode off towards the main part of the hospital.

Joanna was in Richard's thoughts for most of the day and into the evening as well. She was a remarkable woman, an amazingly dedicated nurse and she had stated, without hesitation, that she wanted to go ahead with the divorce as soon as possible. Before their private talk that morning he'd nursed the tiniest hope she might still have some feelings for him. He was not deluded, though, and didn't expect to recapture what they'd once had. He'd thought more in terms of the remnants of their former relationship being intact; a starting point; a foundation from which to rebuild.

It wasn't going to happen.

Joanna had changed, while he was stuck in the past.

So what he had to do was cast away any thoughts of rekindling a personal relationship with his wife and start over.

Today. Right now.

He returned to the ward after the meeting but his and Jo's paths didn't cross again. He focused his attention on his patients.

He spent an hour with an eight-year-old and his parents, explaining stem-cell transplants and answering their many questions. Then he'd been called to deal with a teenager who had developed a dread of her chemotherapy and, for the last two treatments, had started intractable vomiting the night before her three-weekly sessions, in anticipation. She was on the verge of refusing to continue despite an excellent response and it took a lot of persuading to get her to consider coming into the ward as an inpatient to tailor strategies to help her cope. There'd also been two new admissions he made a special effort to see before he left for a hurried, late lunch.

Joanna had been busy with her own duties and, though

he'd been aware of her presence, they hadn't actually spoken again and Richard's afternoon had been a full on session in clinics.

Now he was heading home.

Home...

He'd stay in the apartment until at least the weekend, when he hoped he'd have time to shop for food and the essentials like bed linen that weren't provided as part of the package of his new home. He was looking forward to moving in.

Alone.

If only things had been different.

He drove into the underground car park and headed for the lifts. It wasn't long before he let himself into his apartment and faced the prospect of a long evening with the only company his own. He dumped his briefcase on the coffee table, opened the blinds, exposing a vast expanse of glass and an impressive view of the ocean opposite, and went to the fridge.

He knew exactly how Old Mother Hubbard felt.

There was enough milk left in the half-litre complimentary carton to make a cup of coffee—but he'd used all the coffee. A lonely bottle of mineral water stood next to two bottles of beer, the remains of a six-pack he'd bought on the weekend. Apart from a loaf of stale raisin bread his cupboard was indeed bare.

He reached for a beer, opened it and threw the cap into the bin, the bottle tilting as he did so and dribbling part of its contents onto his hand and the cuff of his shirt. He pulled a couple of tissues from the box on the kitchen counter at the same moment his phone rang.

'Hello, Richard Howell.' He gave the automatic greeting.

'Hi, Dr Howell. It's Jodie.' She paused. 'Remember me? We met this morning.'

Richard's initial response was annoyance. He couldn't

think of any reason a member of the administrative staff would ring him at home on his mobile.

'Yes, I remember. Is there a problem with the house?'

It was the only reason *he* could think of for her after-hours call.

'No, it's nothing to do with that.'

'What, then?'

He thought he could hear the rumbling of voices in the background and then she giggled. He had the fleeting thought it might be a prank and it was the last thing he needed at the end of a long day.

'I know you've only been back at work two days...'

It sounded like she was about to ask him a favour and he took a deep breath.

'Go on.'

'And you may not know that my dad is James Francis and he said he's known you since you were an RMO and that you used to be a member of the hospital jazz band.'

He heard her take a deep breath and tried to make sense of a conversation that was becoming increasingly vague and convoluted. So Jodie was the daughter of Mr Francis, the paediatric surgeon, and, yes, he'd known her father for a long time and they'd jammed together a few times. But when he'd commenced his specialist training at the Stirling then married Joanna within the year, Richard had found the commitment to regular band practice and the occasional charity performance hadn't fitted with the long hours and hectic schedule of a paediatric registrar with a pregnant wife. Most of the other band members had been either old enough to be grandparents or young and unattached. He'd given away music almost completely, although he still had his saxophone.

'And?'

'Um... There's a charity concert planned for the Easter

weekend and the band is without a sax player. Dad suggested contacting you. I know it's over two months away but—'

'No. Thanks for thinking of me but I don't play any more. Even if I wanted to it's been so long and I doubt I'd have the time for regular practice. I was never any good.'

He'd first met Joanna through his music. She'd been in the Stratton University choir and he'd continued to play in what had jokingly been called the Lady Lawler Big Band—more to do with its size than the type of music they'd played, which could range from pop rock to classical as well as traditional jazz. The good old days…

The last thing he needed at the moment was to be reminded of a time in his life that was in his thoughts nearly every day. Playing the saxophone was a rare, solitary activity these days.

'That's not what Dad says. He reckons you're the best saxophone player the band has ever had. Are you doing anything Friday night?'

'Er…' Lord, this woman was pushy, just like her father. He tried to picture the oncology after-hours roster. 'I'm on call.' He was fairly certain Friday and Sunday were his rostered days.

'Perfect. We're having auditions in the B J Cohen Lecture Theatre so if you get a call you'll already be at the hospital.' He heard her clear her throat. 'Not that you need to audition, but it will give you a chance to meet the crew and assess the new talent. What do you say?'

The woman was wearing him down and the idea of getting back to his music had some appeal. Maybe it was meant to be, all part of his new start. There was also the possibility of rescuing his social life, which he'd thought he'd lost for ever.

'Okay. I'll come on Friday, but it doesn't mean I'm committing to playing.'

'Great. Seven-thirty, and bring your saxophone.'

Then she hung up, leaving Richard wondering how she'd managed to persuade him to do something that he really didn't want to do.

The next few days flew by in a blur of ward rounds, clinics, lectures and med-student tutorials. Richard's only contact with Joanna had been on the wards in her capacity as an extremely dedicated and efficient paediatric nurse. There was no doubt in his mind she had a special relationship with her patients and she gave so much more than expected from the job description.

He certainly hadn't had time to think about getting the ball rolling with their divorce but he would try and at least make a couple of phone calls, including one to his solicitor, on his afternoon off the following week.

He packed his briefcase with some paperwork he wanted to take home and then slung his stethoscope on the top before he clicked the case closed.

Friday already.

The reality of committing to even a brief appearance at the concert audition night had been intermittently interrupting his thoughts through the afternoon and now he longed for a quiet evening at home, with a glass of wine, listening to his favourite mood music...*with Joanna snuggled up beside him on the couch.*

An impossible dream.

He sighed as he walked out of Matilda Ward at the end of his first working week. In many ways it was good to be back in Australia; his only disappointment was that the grieving process was beginning again—this time not only for his son but for the demise of his marriage.

Joanna hated being late.

By the time she arrived, there were only a couple of stragglers in the foyer of the lecture theatre—a middle-aged man she didn't recognise who was carrying a cello case and one of the new intake of medical students dressed as an outrageously eccentric clown.

She laughed. The young student stopped and turned around. He'd only been working at Lady Lawler for a few weeks but already had a reputation for his cheeky sense of humour and the occasional practical joke.

'Guess what role I'm up for tonight?' he said in a ridiculously high-pitched voice, but managed a deadpan expression. He waited for her to catch up with him.

'Wow, that's a hard one.' She chuckled. 'It's a long shot but I am guessing it could be the stand-up comedian slot?'

His animated, black-painted lips drooped in an exaggerated expression of despondency as a bright blue tear trickled down one cheek. He whipped out a flamboyant bunch of daisies from somewhere in his baggy trousers and began waving them about as if he were conducting a full symphony orchestra.

'I was hoping for the job of choirmaster.'

Joanna burst into laughter again. He would make a wonderful kids' doctor. An off-beat sense of humour, as long as it was combined with sensitivity, made for ideal qualifications in an aspiring paediatrician.

'Seriously?'

His face lit up again with a grin.

'Seriously,' he repeated, as he made an overstated gesture inviting her to enter the theatre before him. She walked in with a smile on her face, looked around and made her way over towards the section of stage with 'CHOIR' written in broad felt-tip pen on an upended cardboard box. It was part of a disparate set, which seemed to have done the job to guide the hopeful performers to different parts of the stage, depending on their abilities and aspirations.

She waved at the student as he headed towards the section designated 'MISCELLANEOUS'. He was obviously enjoying the attention.

'Good luck,' she called.

But then she stopped dead in her tracks.

She'd been aware of the discordant sound of the various band instruments tuning up but she picked up the strains of a saxophone playing ragtime out of the din. It was a popular Scott Joplin composition but she couldn't remember the name.

Oh, God!

The memories came flooding back.

Why was the saxophonist playing the song Richard had been playing when they'd first met? It must be simply a cruel twist of fate, she thought as she looked over to the crowded band section to see who it was. It certainly didn't sound like Steve, the hospital's long-time player. It wasn't his style.

She scanned the group, telling herself it was simply an unusual coincidence.

Then she saw him.

Richard's unruly hair flopped over his forehead but Joanna could see he had his eyes closed, concentrating fully on the music. He'd always had the ability to focus totally, blocking everything out but the sound of his own instrument. When he finished the lively tune, he stopped and took a deep breath before playing the soulful opening bars of an old traditional jazz ballad called 'Sunset of Sadness'. It was a melody with lyrics about aching hearts, broken promises and shattered dreams. She knew the song by heart. The hummed melody had been a lullaby for Sam during his illness when he'd had trouble getting to sleep. And then, after it had all ended, the song had been comfort for her and Richard when there'd been no other way to express their grief.

Joanna began to mouth the words and then something

strange happened. One by one the other instruments silenced and the rumble of conversation gradually ceased until all that could be heard was the clear, poignant sound of Richard's saxophone. He seemed oblivious to what was happening around him, totally absorbed in the music.

But it was too much for Joanna. The memories stabbed at her heart and silent tears ran down her cheeks. She suddenly felt claustrophobic and had to leave. She stepped off the stage and, head down, walked quietly towards the exit.

But then, in her haste to leave, she stumbled. She grabbed hold of the nearest thing to steady herself. Unfortunately it was a fold-up chair—the top one in a stack leaning against the wall. She fell backwards, taking at least half a dozen metal framed chairs with her.

The music stopped.

The entire occupants of the theatre seemed to take a collective breath before…all hell let loose.

How humiliatingly embarrassing.

The first person to reach her was Richard, closely followed by the clown. At least a dozen concerned faces drifted in and out of her field of vision.

'What happened…?'

'Are you okay…?'

'You've cut your head…'

'Does it hurt anywhere?'

'Did you faint?'

Joanna knew they were well meaning but all she wanted to do at that moment was to escape to somewhere quiet, on her own.

'I'm sure she's okay and I'll take care of her.' Richard's authoritative voice silenced the curious and concerned. 'I think it's best you get back to the auditions.'

With a firm but gentle grip he lifted her to her feet, conveying the message with his eyes that he understood she needed time and space to regain her composure. It was her pride that was injured, not her body. To add insult to injury, she'd exposed her weakness in times of stress, not only to everyone in the lecture theatre but to Richard.

She sniffed, wiped her eyes on the back of her hand and untangled herself from Richard's protective grasp.

'I'm all right. You can go back now,' she said in a voice as unsteady as her wobbly legs.

'What are you going to do?' *His* voice was as steady as a rock.

'I can't stay.'

The expression in Richard's eyes told her he knew why.

'I'm sorry...'

She swallowed, clearing her throat of tears and the rawness of her emotions.

'Don't be. It wasn't your fault. You didn't even know I was there.'

'No,' he said quietly.

She wanted to go home and she also wanted Richard to go away and leave her alone. She felt the shell of her control coming dangerously close to cracking. The way she'd managed her grief and protected herself from painful memories had been to block them out. She couldn't return to that aching place full of sorrow and guilt that had imprisoned her for so long after Sam's death.

She hadn't thought Richard coming back would have this effect, though.

'I'm going home,' she said, reaching up to run her fingers through her hair—before she realised her scalp was covered in less than a week's stubble, and there was something sticky and warm near her ear. She quickly dropped her hand to her side, hoping Richard hadn't noticed. As she turned to leave, Richard grasped her wrist and pulled her around to face him.

'Where do you live? I don't think you should drive. And you need someone to deal with the cut on your head.'

She smiled. Feeling her confidence return, she realised she now had an out.

'I only live around the corner and I walked, so you don't need to worry,' she said defiantly.

'That solves the problem. I can walk with you.'

Maybe it was a culmination of a busy working week, restless nights or possibly a simmering resentment at how easily he'd been persuaded to go public again with his sax playing—whatever the reason, he had become so immersed in the music he hadn't even noticed Joanna arrive.

What on earth had come over him to result in him playing *that* song?

It was a personal and very private part of a past he'd shared with the woman he was certain he'd carelessly hurt badly. No wonder she'd attempted a hasty exit.

'It's not necessary. I told you I only live a street away. I'm quite capable of getting myself home in one piece.'

He wasn't about to be put off by Joanna's stubborn tone. Even if she hadn't stumbled and bumped her head, he firmly believed it wasn't wise for a woman, and certainly not his Joanna, to walk home alone after dark.

She'd already begun to stride ahead of him and he had to quicken his usual brisk pace to catch up. She was definitely a woman with a mission and her mission that night didn't include him.

'I'm only thinking of your safety,' he said tentatively when he caught up. Her protests morphed into a stony silence and he wasn't sure which tactic he liked least. But, thankfully, she wasn't physically pushing him away and the tears he'd noticed earlier had stopped.

They reached the road at the back of the hospital and

stopped at the kerb to wait for traffic to pass. Richard reached out to touch her arm in a gesture he hoped indicated friendship but she shrugged him off.

'How could you?' she said softly as she set off to cross the road at a slow run.

He had no words to explain so he remained silent and several tense minutes later Joanna rounded the corner into a softly-lit street of an odd mix of ancient cottages and more modern multi-storey blocks of flats. He was relieved when she stopped at the gate of one of the cottages.

'This is where I live, so you can go now. I'm quite capable of letting myself in.'

He lingered, not sure how he was going to persuade her to at least let him dress the blood-encrusted wound on her exposed scalp. She'd probably have a decent-sized lump on the back of her head in the morning and she didn't have the luxury of a normal head of hair to disguise it.

'Yes, I know you are, Joanna,' he said with what he hoped she would interpret as compassion. 'But...' It was a difficult decision to make—whether or not to dive in head first and tell her exactly how he felt. He wanted to believe he had nothing to lose but deep down he realised how much was at stake. Joanna didn't hate him—he knew her well enough to be able to gauge the barometer of her feelings—but he understood how much of an upheaval it must have been to have him land back on her doorstep with little time to prepare herself for the disturbing roller-coaster ride he'd forced her to embark on. He decided to try and compromise.

'I can only try and understand how difficult it must be for you, me turning up out of the blue.'

'All the oncology staff were told who was going to take over from Dr Price a couple of weeks after he announced his retirement. It wasn't a total surprise.' Her expression softened and she took a sighing breath. 'I had plenty of time to adjust.'

'So can I at least be your friend?'

'It's not that easy," she said but he didn't want to push her.

'Can we talk inside?'

Richard purposely kept some physical distance between them and hoped Joanna understood he wasn't trying to encroach on her personal space. He didn't want to continue their conversation on the pavement, in the dark, though.

She didn't answer but opened the gate and headed for the pathway running along the side of the building. He began to follow and was relieved she didn't object.

'I live in the house on the back half of the block. It fronts a laneway but I come in this way at night.'

Richard took her comment as a sign she had no objection to him coming with her and continued along the path, a couple of steps behind. By the soft light of the remnants of dusk he could just make out the roofline of a small house tucked behind a two-metre-high fibro fence. Joanna made her way to a second gate and left it open once she had gone through as if she'd resigned herself to the fact that he was tagging along, no matter what she did. A light was on, illuminating the small back patio, and she proceeded to unlock the glass sliding door that led into the rear of her house.

Richard followed her in and glanced around the cluttered living room. There were books piled in a corner, spilling off overloaded shelves. A guitar in a soft case leaned up against the wall next to a music stand holding what looked like a couple of 'how to play' books. The homely furniture was comfortably worn in.

'Sorry about the mess,' Joanna said as she scooped up a basket of washing and stashed it in what he presumed was a laundry room.

'What mess?'

Her response to his attempt at humour was a hard-edged glare as she shifted her roomy shoulder-bag from the coffee table to the counter separating the main living area from a small kitchen.

'Would you like a cup of tea?'

She'd remembered he preferred tea to coffee. It was a small thing but it touched a chord in his heart. She hadn't blotted out all the memories of their past.

'I'd love one.' He paused, wondering if he could penetrate the stubborn resistance she'd demonstrated so far to any help he offered. He decided to take the hard line. 'But after we clean up that wound. There's a fair bit of blood and it's hard to know what's underneath. Have you got a first-aid kit?'

'I'm quite capable of doing it myself,' she said with a scowl.

The hard line hadn't worked so he thought he'd try the practical.

'Maybe if you had eyes in the back of your head. The blood is coming from behind your right ear, so you'd at least need someone to hold a mirror for you. Are you working tomorrow?' As a last resort he thought he'd try and appeal to her sense of vanity. Cosmetically he would certainly do a better job than her, particularly if there was a significant laceration.

She frowned.

They both stood awkwardly at opposite sides of the room as if it was a stand-off. If only she would relax and realise his sole motive was to help her. He'd do the same for a complete stranger. Well, sort of…

'At least go and look in the mirror.'

He began to walk towards her and she edged away like a frightened animal that had been cornered. Was she really so terrified of being alone with him she couldn't bear him to come near her?

'Okay, you win. I'll go and have a look.'

He managed to suppress a gasp as she headed off down a passage that he assumed led to the bedrooms and bathroom. She had a decent-sized haematoma, already an impressive purple colour, on the right side of her occiput and dried blood streaked down her neck. He assumed it would be easy enough to treat the wound but he doubted he could do much to conceal the damage.

He went into the kitchen and opened her freezer, hoping to find something he could improvise as an icepack. His plan was to clean the wound and then apply ice before he attempted any repair work.

'What exactly do you think you're doing?'

Joanna had returned.

He thought of saying something flippant, like he had a sudden craving for ice cream, but he knew better. Joanna wasn't in the mood for jokes.

'An icepack? Can we use the frozen peas?'

She was standing about two metres away, holding a damp, bloodstained face cloth to the back of her head.

'Oh…er…yes, okay.' It wasn't exactly an apology but a step in the right direction.

'What's the verdict? Am I allowed to touch you with my healing hands?'

A hint of a smile crossed her lips and Richard took it as a sign her tension was lessening a little, though he realised he had a long way to go before she'd trust him.

'You're right,' she said, looking everywhere but at his face. 'It's a lot worse than I thought and I doubt I could do a decent job on my own.'

Thank God for that. He had no idea what he would have done if she'd refused.

'Wise decision. To the bathroom, then.'

He followed her down the passage, past two closed doors he assumed were bedrooms to the bathroom. It was efficiently compact, like everything else in the small house, with room enough for a shower recess and vanity. Mirror tiles, topped with a small fluorescent tube, took up most of the wall above the basin. She flicked on the mirror light, laid a first-aid kit and a hospital dressing pack on the vanity.

'There's gauze in the dressing pack, chlorhexidine in a specimen jar and butterfly sutures in the first-aid kit.' The simmering tension ramped up a notch but fortunately wasn't directed at him. 'I just hope it doesn't need stitches,' she added.

'You're certainly well prepared,' he said with a smile, but she'd already turned away from him so he could do his healing work.

'You can take the face cloth off now.' He poured antiseptic into the plastic tray and used the disposable forceps to dab a square of gauze into the bright green liquid. 'Okay if I put a towel over your shoulders?'

Lord, she had beautiful shoulders. They were softly rounded, lightly tanned...

He checked his errant thoughts in double-quick time. There was no point in dwelling on Joanna's physical beauty when he'd been treated like an unpleasant though necessary evil as soon as they'd walked through her door.

She reached across for the hand towel next to the vanity and draped it across her upper back as if she'd suddenly become aware of the amount of skin exposed by her strappy singlet top. She was obviously keen for him to get on with the job in hand so she could reclaim her territory.

'Right, then. This might sting a little.' Richard rolled out the standard hospital-speak.

She remained silent but he could see her tension as he applied the cool liquid to clean the skin around the wound before discarding it. He doubted his ministrations would be painful so she was most likely responding to his touch. He disposed of the soiled gauze and began cleaning the wound with a fresh swab.

'It's only small,' he said, to reassure himself as much as

Joanna. 'About a centimetre. One butterfly suture should be enough to close the wound and I expect it will be healed in three or four days.' He ran his fingers over the boggy skin covering the haematoma. 'The bruising will take longer, though.' He chuckled. 'It's quite a work of art.'

'Just get on with it.' Richard could feel her disapproval. 'Please,' she added quietly.

Oh, how Joanna wanted him to hurry up and finish so she could send him packing. The last thing she needed was to experience Richard Howell, one-time husband extraordinaire, up close and personal.

The problem was that her reaction to him had been totally unexpected.

She'd thought she was over him, but she had been wrong.

When she'd seen him at the auditions and then heard *that* song, the memories had been like a bunch of sharp needles pricking her head, trying to penetrate her brain. And she'd managed to ward them off, keep them at an acceptable distance, until Richard insisted he accompany her home.

It wasn't his fault either. He was just being the same caring, loving, gentle man he'd always been. She was the one who had changed. She'd spent the past three years making a new life for herself with a thickly drawn line separating it from her past. Seeing Richard again meant reliving the deep, unremitting pain of losing their darling son and the cruel way she'd rejected her husband during her grieving. She was the one who'd destroyed their marriage by shrouding herself in a cocoon of sorrow. Richard had done the right thing in leaving her and he deserved a new life too...without her. He had to move on, not live in the past, and for him to achieve some sort of closure she knew she mustn't let him get close to her.

'Ouch!'

She was brought back to reality by the sharp pain of strong

fingers holding her wound together while the butterfly suture was carefully applied. Richard was leaning close and she could feel the comforting warmth of his steady breathing on her neck.

'I thought you were going to ice it first.'

'I changed my mind. The laceration's smaller than I thought.'

She turned around to face him, being careful not to put any tension on the wound. His eyes twinkled with amusement. *Dangerous.*

He was making it difficult for her to maintain the distance she desperately needed to... To what? To stop herself falling into his comforting arms? To stop the mesmerising look in his eyes from melting her resolve? To stop him from unravelling her tightly ordered world that didn't have room in it for a man, let alone a man who'd done everything he could to help her through the biggest tragedy in her life, the only thanks he'd had to be coldly rejected.

If there was still a tiny spark of attraction it was purely physical. He was a very good-looking, sexy man and she'd not shared her bed, in fact she'd not had a boyfriend, since Richard had left. Sex wasn't the basis of a long-term relationship, though. There had to be commitment, and that was asking the impossible of her. There was no denying her happiest days had been with Richard and Sam but she couldn't face the prospect of having to relive the anguish when things had gone wrong. She'd been so young. She'd had dreams of a perfect life. Now she knew there were no guarantees of happily ever after, but there were certain precautions she could take to minimise the possibility of being hurt.

She moved away from him.

'Thanks,' she said quietly as she collected the debris of the clean-up and placed it in the bin.

'My pleasure,' he said, still smiling. 'I'll go and make tea, shall I?'

I'll go and make tea.

The simple statement tripped a switch for Joanna. Tears rolled down her cheeks and she began to sob.

It had always been Richard's solution when the road had been rough or they'd had a disagreement—to make a cup of tea, sit down quietly and not make any decisions until they'd at least finished one cup. But she didn't need to be reminded.

She sniffed, but before she managed to bring her hand up to her eyes to wipe away the evidence of memories she'd tried to put behind her, Richard enfolded her in his arms. And she was powerless to resist. She felt the steady thud of his heart-beat, the gentle movement of his chest with each breath, the solid, reassuring strength of his arms around her, the feather touch of his lips on her forehead.

'No!'

No way. The stakes were too high. She couldn't bear even the slightest possibility of heartache all over again.

Richard dropped his arms as she pulled away.

'What's the matter, Jo?'

She wiped away the remains of her tears with a handful of tissues and blew her nose.

'Nothing's the matter. I'll be all right in a few minutes.' She took a deep breath to steady her voice. 'I don't want tea after all. I need to be on my own.'

The cold stare she sent him did the job and he gathered the jacket he'd shed before attending to her injury.

'Are you sure you're okay?'

'I'm fine,' she almost growled.

'Right. I'll see you at work next week, then.' He opened the sliding door, the lines on his face indicating a mixture of bewilderment and concern. At the last moment he turned. 'I'm sorry, I didn't mean to—'

'Just go,' she said, and closed the door firmly behind him.

CHAPTER FOUR

When Richard arrived back at the hospital the auditions were in full swing. He couldn't face going back in, though. And he was too emotionally drained to even talk on the phone to James Francis. So he decided to leave a message at the switchboard, requesting them to contact his colleague and ask him if he could look after his saxophone until Monday.

Maybe by then he would be in a fit state to apologise and explain.

Maybe his busy weekend—shopping, moving into his new house, going through the motions of settling in—would take his mind off the disturbing thoughts of Joanna that wouldn't leave his head.

But it didn't.

He was still thinking of her when he arrived on the ward early Monday morning to do a quick check of the weekend admissions. When he found out Joanna wasn't starting until nine it was difficult to disguise his disappointment.

A busy morning in the long-term follow-up clinic at least cheered him up and gave him something outside himself and his inner confusion to concentrate on. The morning was taken up with seeing the happy, living evidence of all the hard work his team did in the early stages of diagnosing and treating childhood cancer.

It always gratified him to know more than eighty per cent

of his charges survived their disease for longer than five years and the majority of those went on to live normal adult lives. All of the patients he saw that morning had done well: Jenna, who'd had a brain tumour removed as a baby, now a lively toddler; Jay and Tom, two young adults who'd been the same age when they'd developed osteogenic sarcomas affecting the tibia, a bone in the lower leg. Tom had needed amputation but Jay's leg had been saved. Though the boys lived in different parts of the state they'd stayed friends and always organised their clinic visits for the same time. And, of course, the majority of leukaemia victims did well.

When he waved the last patient out the door, Richard packed his things.

'See you next time,' Margaret, the sister in charge, called as he headed towards the door. 'Have a good afternoon.'

'I'll try,' he replied, feeling an unexpected jolt of nerves at the prospect of seeing Joanna again.

He had a quick lunch and headed for Matilda Ward for the first round of the week—a teaching round. He expected it to be demanding because it included the junior doctors as well as two or three medical students.

And Joanna would be there.

If his first working week was anything to go by, the ward rounds she attended always seemed to have an air of cheerfulness. She could be counted on to lighten the atmosphere if either staff or patients got bogged down in the sometimes daunting complexities of the diseases and their treatment.

If there was a bright side, she'd find it.

And there she was. He could see her through the glass partition enclosing the day ward, where procedures like outpatient chemotherapy, lumbar punctures and transfusions were performed. Her eyes were bright with encouragement as she assisted with supervision of three children having chemo. Though he couldn't hear what she was saying, one of her charges laughed and the others were smiling at her animated conversation.

He held up his hand in what could be interpreted as either a wave or a truce, but she ignored him and continued her jovial chat with the kids.

Did the woman have endless reserves of strength? he wondered as he swung into the nurses' station, almost colliding with Anita, the resident.

'Sorry, I was just coming to find you,' she said. She'd only been working on the unit a couple of weeks but Lynne had told him she'd already proved to be keen, competent and a quick learner.

'What can I do for you?'

She looked a little put out, as if she was about to ask for bus fare to the moon.

'I need supervision inserting a central line. Jack's in Theatre with Tilly Farmer and the plastics team.' Jack was one of the oncology registrars in his final year of specialist training, trying to learn everything he could and hoping for an overseas posting when he'd finished his exams. The young doctor took a long sighing breath. 'And this one will make up my quota so I can officially do them on my own.'

Richard glanced at his watch. He had twenty-five minutes before the round was due to start.

'Is it set up?'

'In the chemo suite. Joanna said she's available to help if I need her.'

Right.

Joanna was available.

Terrific. Wasn't it? Of course it was. She was the best nurse on the ward and he wouldn't let the unresolved issues he had with her distract him.

'And the patient?'

'Danny Sims.'

'He's an outpatient, isn't he? Pelvic Ewing's sarcoma.'

'That's right,' the resident doctor said as they walked towards the specially set-up suite of cubicles. 'Dr Price prescribed intensive initial therapy in view of the site and prognosis.'

The boy's diagnosis made working with Joanna even more difficult as Danny had the same type of cancer that had taken Sam's life. He wondered how Joanna would cope. Would she relive a little of the pain of Sam's illness every time she saw Danny?

Richard remembered seeing Alan Price's notes on the boy and the chemo regime he'd worked out. Though cures were increasingly common for the extremely rare but often fast-growing tumour of the connective tissue associated with bone, location in the pelvic area meant a much poorer prognosis.

'When's he due to start treatment?'

'Not until tomorrow but if we put in the catheter this afternoon, he should be able to start first thing in the morning. He's staying overnight.' She smiled as they entered the wash room where they scrubbed up. 'Of course Dr Price asked that you review him before we start. I was going to ask you to look at his notes this afternoon after the round and get Jack to supervise—'

'But he's in Theatre, for a long haul.'

'Probably all afternoon. And Pharmacy needs the okay today to make up his drug regime.'

'No problem. Let's go and say hello to Danny, then.'

Richard was pleased to find out the thirteen-year-old patient and his father, who looked more nervous than the boy, had been well prepared. Anita had explained exactly what would be done and Danny had been given a mild sedative by one of the nurses as soon as it was confirmed the procedure was to go ahead.

Richard introduced himself.

'I'm Dr Richard Howell, the specialist who will be looking after you from now on. Anita is going to put a tiny plastic tube into one of the large veins in your chest so you can have the amount and type of drugs you need without having to have a new line each time you come in.'

'Will it hurt?' Danny said drowsily.

'A little,' Anita answered with a smile. 'You'll feel the needle with the local anaesthetic like a pinprick, but that will make the skin go numb.'

Richard turned when he heard the curtains of the cubicle part.

'Hi, champ,' Joanna said cheerfully, as if she had known Danny for years. Richard's worries about any difficulties she might have coping were immediately allayed. 'And I checked up about…ahem.' Joanna made a theatrical show of clearing her throat. 'That very special person *is* coming to the ward on the day you have your second treatment, but you mustn't tell a soul I told you. It's supposed to be a big surprise,' she added with a wink, and Danny managed a grin.

'Our secret,' he said.

She nodded in the direction of Danny's father. 'Jenny's with the kids today, is she, Pete?'

He nodded and then paled, looking as if he was about to faint.

'It's getting a bit crowded in here. Why don't you go and make yourself a cuppa in the parents' room?' she said tactfully, glancing in Richard's direction for his approval to give Pete an excuse to leave. He nodded, aware that their young patient's anxiety level had definitely ebbed after Joanna had appeared. 'Okay, Danny?'

The teenager's eyes had drifted closed and he opened them briefly, managing the slightest smile. 'Yeah, you go, Dad, but you'll stay, won't you, Sister?'

She patted his leg. 'Of course. Someone has to keep an eye on these doctors. Is that okay with you guys?' she asked.

She was in total control, treating Richard like a consultant she was working with, behaving exactly as she should be. Maybe he'd blown out of proportion her almost hostile reaction to him on Friday night. She was certainly better at filing away the past than he was.

'Fine by me,' Richard said, trying to adopt the same attitude, which hovered somewhere between professional and friendly-casual.

'Good.'

Joanna peeled open another set of sterile surgical gloves and then tilted the bed head down to help fill Danny's chest and neck veins. She went off to wash her hands while Anita carefully swabbed the skin of the right side of the boy's torso.

'Feeling all right?' Anita asked, but Danny seemed to be drifting in and out of a light sleep, a sign of effective sedation. There was a good chance he wouldn't even remember the catheter insertion.

Joanna returned and slipped her hands into her gloves.

'I'll just watch and let me know if you want any help or advice,' Richard said as he moved back from the bed and stood where he had a good view of the two women at work.

Anita anaesthetised the skin just below the clavicle then made a small cut to locate the subclavian vein, which sits beneath the bone but in front of the artery. Joanna dabbed at the small wound and placed a finger in the notch at the top of the breastbone so that Anita could line up the needle at the correct angle. Insertion of the plastic tube into the vein and its tunnelling under the skin went smoothly, a good back flow of blood indicating it was likely to be in the correct position. A small cuff on the tube was inflated to help keep it in place under the skin and an X-ray would confirm it was in the right place and that no damage had been done to the underlying lung.

'Well done.' Richard checked the time. 'Can I leave you to suture, check Danny's chest and organise radiology? I'll speak to Danny's father before he leaves.'

'Yes. And thanks, Dr Howell.'

'I'll see you on the ward round when you've finished.'

Richard was only five minutes late to the round and Anita joined him and his group not long after, but he noticed Joanna's absence.

'Isn't Sister Raven joining us this afternoon?' he asked Lynne quietly when they were walking between patients.

'No, she's working in the chemo suite until the day cases finish. It's better she stays there. Is there a problem?' He chose to ignore the curious look in the charge sister's eyes.

'No, of course not. It's just that…'

'She brightens your day?'

Yes, that's exactly right, he thought. She's like a ray of sunshine generously shedding light and warmth wherever she goes.

'She brightens everyone's day,' he conceded to say with a pleasant but what he hoped was detached smile as they reached a grizzling toddler in a cot.

'Hello, Mrs Bryant.' The child's mother looked over-wrought and overtired. Now was not the time to enquire how she was coping and he made a mental note to call back and see her at the end of the round.

'Would you mind if Travis…' he indicated one of the medical students '…gently examines Taylor's tummy?'

The child had a Wilm's tumour, a cancer arising from the kidney, and often presented as an abdominal mass. She was undernourished and being fed by a nasogastric tube in order to try and improve her general condition prior to surgery the following week.

'All right,' Liz Bryant said with a sigh, but she moved protectively towards her daughter and began to stroke her head.

Travis completed the examination awkwardly, one of his hands big enough to span the child's abdomen from side to side.

'I'd like to come back and see you later on my own,' Richard said quietly.

She picked up her crying child and rocked Taylor in her arms. She nodded then turned her back on the group and walked to the window. Richard wished Joanna was available to comfort her and realised, after one short week back in Matilda Ward he had begun to take her bubbly, happy, caring presence for granted. He was coming to depend on her being there for her tireless ability to comfort and offer hope in the grimmest situations.

He missed her…

He wanted part of the joy she spread for himself.

'Come on,' he said with enthusiasm. 'Let's head for the tutorial room. Don't think you can get out of it. Alan told me he'd asked one of you to prepare a case presentation.'

There was a general chuckle from the group as they followed him down the corridor and out of the ward.

Richard wasn't like some of the other hospital consultants who would rather starve than go to the canteen, but sometimes, like this afternoon, he wanted solitude during his breaks. The couple of times he'd had lunch in the busy dining hall, hoping to see Joanna, he'd found himself bullied into sitting with a group of chattering nurses, at least one of whom would decide to flirt with him.

Not that there was anything wrong with nurses, or chattering, or flirting, but if it continued unremittingly he knew it would wear him down. If he'd been ten years younger he would have been flattered but he had matured and was past all that now.

So after the tutorial he'd headed for the public coffee shop, which he knew was rarely frequented by staff. He needed a few minutes time-out before he went back to Matilda to tidy up loose ends and leave his work in the ward in order for the evening staff. That had always been his way of coping with the stress of never seeming to have enough time in the day—pacing himself; not succumbing to time pressure or being hurried; not leaving a job half-done, hoping others would pick up the pieces.

It was close to closing time so he wasn't surprised to see he was the sole customer and ordered a flat white—it was the only place you could get a decent coffee in the hospital—and chose a quiet table hidden from the entrance but with a view of the passing parade going in and out of the main hospital block.

When he'd seen Joanna coming out of the nurses' amenities building and heading his way he'd assumed she was on her way home but Marnie—the woman had introduced herself the first time he'd visited the shop—must have seen him looking at her.

She'd set his drink down and said, 'She's one of the few who are brave enough to go all the way.'

He hadn't quite understood what she meant.

'Sorry?'

'The full shave.'

'Oh, I see what you mean.'

'She'll have a cappuccino. I'll put money on it.'

'If she comes in and asks for one, let me buy. I work with her and I wouldn't mind some company.'

The woman's eyes widened fractionally and then she smiled as if they were plotting a secret revolution together.

'Okay.' She sashayed back to the counter.

A few seconds later Joanna *did* come into the shop and although Richard couldn't see her he could hear the conversation. The muscles of his jaw tightened just a little and he unconsciously began tapping his saucer with his spoon. He seriously wanted to share a drink with Joanna, enjoy her smile and her honey-smooth voice. And if it was only work they talked about, that would be okay. He realised he'd be more than disappointed if she refused. So when Marnie started rambling on about secret admirers he felt he had to show himself. He'd set up the situation, and there was no room for second thoughts.

There were only a few kids Joanna came back to visit after-hours and she was careful not to give the impression she had any favourites. She knew how attached many of the sick and frightened children could become to a staff member who gave that little bit extra. She was lucky she had plenty to give but made sure she rationed her off-duty time and energy with care.

She couldn't help what she felt for young Danny Sims, though. It would take a miracle to cure him; she knew from firsthand experience the odds were stacked miserably against him.

When Sam had been diagnosed with Ewing's, Richard's knowledge of paediatrics hadn't been enough for her. She'd read everything she could get her hands on about the disease that had been threatening the life of her son, from scientific, evidence-based research to personal anecdotes on the internet. Even testimonials about farfetched miracle cures. She remembered one of the few times Richard had become frustrated with her emotional attempts to cling to increasingly fading hopes. He'd accused her of clutching at straws and it had probably been the first tiny step at the fork in the road—where she'd begun to reject him.

If she could turn back the clock... If she knew what she did now...

Richard had been trying to cope in his own way.

She'd seen only one case of Ewing's since she'd been working on Matilda and the boy, a couple of years older than Sam, who had just turned six when he passed away, had miraculously survived and was in remission.

But Danny Sims's case was different.

For a start, his chances of getting the disease in the first place were roughly the same as winning Lotto. And if you ticked the boxes of the features of the teenager's cancer that were associated with a poor prognosis, he would probably score a six or seven out of ten.

But Joanna's philosophy was that there was always hope, exceptions to those horribly inhuman statistics. Miracles did happen, and if they didn't, Joanna always tried her best to make the road less bumpy for the unfortunate few in her surrogate brood.

If she couldn't have children of her own, she'd decided, she'd devote that instinctive maternal part of herself to her job—caring for kids with cancer.

She had completed her nursing degree during her pregnancy and graduated a month before the baby was due. Then she'd put her career on hold while she'd been a full-time mum. She'd planned to go back nursing when Sam started school, but it hadn't happened. Her son's illness had been diagnosed when Sam had been in pre-school and he'd survived only eleven heart-breaking months.

Making the decision to go back to work had been a turning point for her once she'd managed to control her grief and had been sure Richard wasn't coming back. It had been an easy decision to extend her nursing qualifications to include oncology. The last two years had been immensely satisfying.

And now Richard was back...well...there was no reason

anything should change other than formalising their separation with a divorce.

I am a good nurse, I love the children I care for and that's all that matters.

'That's all that matters,' she repeated in a whisper to reinforce the words she'd found herself repeating several times over the weekend when troubling thoughts of her husband had kept steamrolling into the peaceful solitude of her days off.

Thank goodness it was Monday afternoon and she'd finished her shift. She planned to call back and see Danny and Taylor as well as Raymond, a new admission who'd looked scared to death when he'd come in but she hadn't had a chance to have a *proper* talk to him. Then she'd buy some take-away for dinner, head home and spend a quiet evening watching a DVD. Relaxing. Unwinding from her hectic day.

She changed into jeans and a T-shirt, slipped out of her sensible black lace-ups and into low-heeled sandals, deciding to head for the hospital shop. She might even treat herself to the luxury of a cappuccino in a real china cup before she hit the wards again. At least once a week she enjoyed checking out the magazines as well, so she knew what was stocked in-house if one of her patients who needed cheering up had a passion for soccer or horseriding or fashion. Small, personal things could make a big difference.

She breezed into the shop.

'Hi, Jo. Love the five-o'clock-shadow look,' Marnie, the woman in charge of the coffee shop cum newsagent cum florist said with a smile. Joanna was finally becoming used to her bald look but the comments still came in abundance, especially about the bump that at least now was reducing in size. She ran her palm across the stubble on the top of her head.

'Like it? Maybe I'll keep it this short. It's certainly easy to care for.'

'Don't you dare. You've got beautiful hair. Finished for the day?' she added.

'Yes, thank goodness. It's been a long one.' She wasn't about to tell Marnie that it was partly due to the trouble she'd had sleeping the last couple of nights.

'We all have those but in your job you probably get more than your fair share.'

'Mmm…'

Joanna began flipping through a magazine on home renovation. It had caught her eye because on the cover was a photo of a house that looked uncannily like the house she'd lived in with Richard and Sam; the house she'd loved and had had every intention of spending the rest of her days in.

The best-laid plans, she thought with more than a hint of world-weary cynicism.

'There's a special on cappuccino today.' Joanna could tell her friend was about to come out with a friendly jibe. If the shop was empty Marnie would sometimes give her a second cup free of charge. That was usually when she couldn't hide her tiredness or the fact she'd had a particularly difficult day. Perhaps the prison hairstyle made her look gaunt and contributed to the *poor me, I need some comfort* look. She hoped that she wasn't so transparent that even Marnie could see right through her.

'Oh, yeah?' she said with a grin as she placed the glossy on the counter. 'I'm going to treat myself. What was that about the coffee?'

'On the house, sort of. I've got instructions from a secret admirer.' The middle-aged woman giggled like a schoolgirl and Joanna wasn't sure she'd heard correctly.

'Pardon, what did you say?'

Marnie's gaze fixed on something behind her and Joanna turned to see, of all people, Richard emerge from behind a large display of dried flowers. If she hadn't been so surprised, she would have laughed. He and Marnie were looking at each other conspiratorially.

'What's all this about?' Joanna asked, with a sudden urge to turn around and head out the way she'd come in.

'I'll leave it to the doctor to explain. Coffee for two, I presume.'

'Thanks,' Richard said as he led Joanne to a table by a large window at the back of the shop.

She wondered if it was more than coincidence that she kept bumping into him at every turn.

'Richard…er…what a surprise,' Joanna said with a twinkle of what Richard assumed was amusement in her eyes. She was definitely more relaxed than the last time he'd seen her outside the workplace.

'Just needed a break and some real coffee for a change. I thought you'd finished for the day.'

She certainly looked different in her civvies. The clingy, watermelon-pink T-shirt, scooped low at the neckline, highlighted the delicious fact that she had generous curves but in all the right places. And she had gorgeous legs, snugly denim-clad and stretching right up to… She was as beautiful as the day he'd met her.

'Please sit down and join me.'

'Thanks.'

'I thought as soon as you downed tools you'd be heading off to relax.'

A wayward hand went up in the direction of her hair. Nervous? It was the only indication she gave. He smiled.

'Phantom hair?' He couldn't resist the jibe. The conversation was flowing smoothly and he didn't want the tone to change, not just yet.

'Pardon?' she said, obviously not understanding his light-hearted remark.

'You know, like a phantom leg. A person who's had an amputation can still experience sensations like itching or pain where the limb used to be.' He paused, waiting for a response, but her face was expressionless. 'You have phantom hair,' he repeated.

'Oh, I get it,' she conceded, but concentrated all her attention on making patterns with her spoon in the froth in her cup.

'So why aren't you heading off for some down-time?'

She looked up and stared straight into his eyes, as if deciding whether it was worth the effort to reply with the sort of explanation she assumed he wanted to hear, or take the simpler option of telling the truth.

'Sometimes I visit a particular child, or parent even, as a friend, when I'm off duty. It's not easy to spend the time with them they need if you've got dressings to do, medications to give. You know what I mean. I particularly wanted to see Danny.'

'Danny,' he repeated softly. Of course she'd want to do everything she could for Danny and his family. She would know that his chances of getting through the next year or two were slim. His cancer had already spread.

'He's staying overnight…but of course you know,' she added, flushing slightly.

'Yes.'

He wanted to ask her if she was okay, but he wouldn't. It wasn't the time or place. He guessed no one else in the hospital knew about her past, about Sam. And he had to respect that.

Marnie appeared with more coffee.

'Sorry I took so long,' she said with a grin. 'Everyone decided to come at once.' She glanced over at a table where a family of four sat with what looked like a mountain of sandwiches, cakes and bottled soft drinks. 'Can I get you anything else?'

Richard shook his head and glanced at his companion.

'Nothing for me,' she said.

He pushed his empty cup out of the way and began absently stirring his fresh one.

Joanna was silent. Uncomfortable maybe?

'I wanted to have a word with the Simses as well. And Taylor Bryant's mum seemed...' He stopped to think for a moment.

'Depressed?'

Not only was Joanna insightful but she really cared.

'That's what I thought too.'

'She told me she'd had postnatal depression after Taylor was born, and recovered. She'd been doing really well until...' She was much more comfortable talking about work.

'The books tell us that parents experience a process of grieving when their child is diagnosed with a chronic illness, and cancer is the worst scenario. But in the real world no case is the same.' Richard suddenly realised he was talking to someone who had gone through it all. And he'd been there with her. He'd shared the shock and denial, the anger and finally acceptance long after the diagnosis had been made. The knowledge he'd had as a paediatrician in training hadn't made it any easier. In fact, it had probably made it worse. And then they'd experienced it all again when Sam had died. He wished he'd kept his big mouth shut.

'Sorry,' he added.

She looked at him for a long moment, the pupils of her striking black-brown eyes dilating a fraction before she spoke.

'Don't be,' she finally said. 'I'm okay with it.' Her eyes moved to focus on a place in the distance before they returned to fix on his. 'I'll never get over it. I don't think any parent who has to cope with what I...*we*...did does. But we all heal in different ways. I'm sorry I made it so hard for you. I know you tried to be there for me but I just couldn't believe anyone, not even you, could understand. I needed to work through the whole process on my own.'

She'd been fiddling with her spoon, rotating it on the table, but she stopped and surprised him by reaching over and laying her hand on his.

'Like you said, people cope in different ways. And that was my way. Alone.' She paused to take a sighing breath. 'I've got a good but very different life now. And I wouldn't want it any other way.' She gave him the same sort of soothing smile she bestowed on grieving parents and confused kids.

'Look I didn't mean to—'

'We had to talk about it. I thought there might be problems with you worrying how I would deal with Danny. It needed to come out in the open. I'll cope.' Her hand went up to her head again. 'And you don't have to worry about my personal history interfering with my work. I make sure it doesn't.'

Richard wanted to talk some more on a different level, to reassure her and tell her how brave she was and that there was no one in the world like her, but he knew anything he said would be a clichéd pat on the back and he wasn't sure how to open his heart without hurting her even more.

'I don't doubt it for a moment,' he finally said. 'I've been back long enough to see how you work and I've no complaints.'

Joanna sipped her coffee.

'I'm a bit of a cappuccino junkie. This is good, but I really must go.'

She stood, leaving half her drink.

'You're going to Maltilda?'

'That's right.'

'To see Danny and his dad?'

'Yeah.'

'Mind if I come with you?'

She smiled again and the warmth of it enveloped him like a curative hug. It was like the old days but he knew he'd have to work hard at keeping Joanna on his side.

'Of course not. We're playing on the same team after all.'

She was right. And for once in his life he believed winning was important, not just how you played the game.

CHAPTER FIVE

THEY visited Danny together and Richard learned a lot about his young patient and a little more about *the new, independent* Joanna. And what he discovered, he liked…a lot.

She seemed to have a natural rapport with teenagers by somehow tapping into that unique kind of humour that allowed them to stick a finger up at authority but at the same time laugh at themselves. The haircut definitely helped. He knew he was being selfish but an image of those stunning, lustrous locks haunted him as he put his signature to the last patient folder, filed it away and stood up to leave.

After he left the ward, picked up his saxophone from the receptionist in the department of surgery, bought enough food from the deli opposite the hospital to put together a light meal and headed for home.

Home?

It was a house full of someone else's furniture he didn't particularly like; a house decorated in sombre, neutral colours he would never have chosen himself; and, in a weird subliminal way, it reminded him of the hospital.

It was a comfortable two-storey terrace house that would fill the gap nicely until he found a place of his own, but nothing more. He doubted he would ever think of it as home.

He rinsed his plate under the tap and left it on the draining board, poured himself a glass of wine and settled on the sofa. Withdrawing his hand midway on its journey to the TV remote control, he sighed. He'd always believed that watching television was what you resorted to when you had neither the motivation nor energy to do anything else. He'd watched a lot of TV in England but he'd used the excuse that it was often late at night after working a twelve-hour day and a way of turning off his brain from the highs and lows of his job. He didn't want to get into that same rut and one of his New Year resolutions had been to *make time* in his hectic schedule for two things—exercise and socialising, preferably involving an activity that combined the two.

His first dalliance into meeting people—the concert auditions—had been a failure. During his first week at Lady Lawler, despite the abundance of eligible and attractive females, he'd not had the slightest inclination to ask a single one of them out. Even if he had fancied any of the hospital staff, he felt so out of practice when it came to dating, he doubted he'd have the courage to ask.

Knockbacks hurt.

He was in the process of wading through the result of the ultimate knockback—a divorce—and he didn't really want to visit that place again any time soon.

So that left exercise.

He got up, went to his bedroom and rummaged in the bag of new purchases, retrieving a large, fluffy, navy-blue bath towel. Then he found the chlorine-faded swimming trunks he'd taken with him to the U.K. but had hardly worn. He threw them both in a small backpack he used for hand luggage when travelling by plane, grabbed a handful of change, his car keys and headed outside.

Swimming was the most restful form of exercise Joanna knew. Up until Richard had mentioned joining a gym with a lap pool, she'd forgotten how soothing cutting through cool water, stroke by rhythmic stroke, could be. One of the things Richard had insisted on was that their son learn to swim at an early age.

'We live in a country surrounded completely by water. Australia has some of the most beautiful...and treacherous... beaches in the world.' Richard's words echoed in Joanna's mind. 'He doesn't have to be a champion swimmer, just fit and strong enough in the water to be safe. Or as safe as he can be.'

They'd started him in the baby classes at the local public pool and he'd taken to the water with the grace and playfulness of a dolphin. He'd loved swimming, just like his father. A month before his fifth birthday he'd been accepted into the Seals Squad with the distinction of being the youngest member of the group. Richard's heart had almost burst with pride. It had been a father-and-son activity and attending Sam's swimming meets had been something Richard had always seemed to be able to make time for.

Because of Richard's work commitments, Joanna had usually been the one to take Sam to training, though. One of the high points of her week had been the twenty minutes she spent with him simply having fun in the water before the formal session began.

Sam had endearingly called it his warm-up, probably so as not to lose face with his pint-sized mates by admitting he enjoyed mucking about in the pool with his mum.

As well as regular visits to the pool, on every warm Sunday Richard had had off work, they'd gone to the beach. They'd taken Sam to the beach the week before he'd died. It had been a heart-wrenching experience for Joanna to see her husband gently carry their fragile son to the water's edge and ease him into the calm sea of the bay until they had been waist deep. Over the many years they'd been coming to the coast, a pod of dolphins had appeared, probably half a dozen times.

Miraculously the dolphins had come that day, swimming quietly and with unprecedented curiosity. They'd actually come close enough for Richard to guide his son's hand to touch one of them.

It had been the last time Joanna had seen her son laugh.

She'd been convinced they'd come to say goodbye.

And it had been the last time she and Richard had shared the raw emotion of the love they had for their precious child. Tears had been streaming down Richard's face when he'd emerged from the shallows. Tears that had dried up and been replaced by solid calm.

The memories flooded back.

They'd been the perfect family, living a perfect life.

She'd often thought Sam had been growing up too quickly. But then he'd had his childhood stolen from him...

At the age of six years and four months.

A tear trickled down her cheek as she smoothed the electric-blue one-piece swimsuit she'd chosen to wear in preference to the way-too-revealing ice-white bikini Richard had bought her for their fourth wedding anniversary—along with a wonderful romantic holiday to Coral Bay. She scrunched up the garments and jammed them back into the corner of her underwear drawer then opened the door of her wardrobe and looked in the full-length mirror. She straightened her back, pulled in her stomach and had fleeting second thoughts that she knew she mustn't let take hold.

'If I don't do it now, I never will,' she muttered as she pulled on shorts and a T-shirt, grabbed her bag and headed out the front door.

The pool was a couple of kilometres away from where she lived, far enough away for Joanna to take her car.

When she pulled into the parking area of the recreation centre Joanna could hear the booming music of an aerobic dance class and nearly collided with a family group tumbling out of a people-mover van that pulled up next to her.

'Sorry,' she said as she jammed herself flat against her car door to let the four children pass, and almost succumbed to an impulse to get back into her car and drive home.

'No, I can do it,' she whispered with new resolve. She needed the exercise, she loved swimming and coming back to where she had spent so many happy hours with Sam she hoped would be cathartic.

'What did you say? Were you talking to me?'

Joanna looked up to see a woman carrying a large bundle of towels and what appeared to be various floaties and pool toys suitable for pre-school-aged children. The driver, who Joanna assumed was the children's father, was already halfway to the entrance of the recreation complex with three children of various ages and sizes following. The youngest straddled his shoulders.

The woman looked vaguely familiar.

Joanna smiled. 'No I'm just talking to myself.'

The woman was now out of the car and staring at her.

'Joanna? Joanna Howell? Your hair—I hardly recognised you.'

Joanna squinted, trying to make out the stranger's features in the half-light of the electric lamps illuminating the car park.

'Sorry, do I know you?'

'It's Teresa. Teresa Deleo. Angie and Sam used to swim together.' She chuckled. 'And your Richard and my Rick used to be way more competitive than the kids ever were. We used to get so embarrassed.' Her expression turned serious. 'I wanted to contact you after…er…Sam passed away, but Rick said it was too soon. That seeing our kids might upset you. And then we heard you'd gone overseas.'

Her friend had got it wrong but Joanna didn't have the energy to explain that it had only been Richard who had moved away. That they'd separated. It was way too personal to go into the details in the leisure centre car park.

Suddenly Teresa's arms were around Joanna's shoulders, embracing her in a heartfelt hug. It felt so good—the unconditional hug of an old friend.

At the beginning, Joanna hadn't intentionally avoided the friends she'd made through play group, then pre-school and school. There hadn't seemed to be common ground any more. It had been a time when she definitely couldn't have coped with the well-meaning gestures of a group of mothers where the glue of their friendship was their children. It had been partly her fault. She'd shrugged off the phone calls and occasional visits with the often brusque explanation that she was coping as best she could, in her own way, and she didn't need their help. After a few months they'd given up trying to contact her.

At the time she'd wondered why Teresa hadn't got in touch.

Teresa dropped her hands and took a step back. Joanna was suddenly aware of the chill of the night air and shivered. Her companion noticed.

'Hey, let's go inside and then we can chat.'

Joanna felt oddly off balance as she obediently followed Teresa through the car park to the entry of the large public leisure centre and the pool area beyond. Her friend chatted continuously, asking questions and not seeming to require answers, but it had the effect of distracting Joanna from her own demons, which had come close to sending her running home with her tail between her legs.

'Shall we go out to the play pools where the kids are?' She smiled. 'Or are you seriously into fitness?'

'I have to admit I haven't been here since…' Somehow she couldn't finish the sentence with the painful truth. Teresa paused and sensed her discomfort.

'Oh, I'm so sorry,' she said quietly. 'Of course, I should have kept my big mouth shut. How could I have been so insensitive?'

In all the years Jo had known Teresa, she had never seen her blush, but her cheeks were glowing crimson now. In a roundabout way, her friend's discomfort helped Joanna regain her own composure.

'There's no need to apologise. In fact, I'm glad we bumped into each other. I was close to chickening out and going home.'

They'd reached the noisy area where twenty or so small children were competing with each other to see who could make the most noise. Interspersed were a half a dozen supervising adults, including Teresa's husband. He was a big, hirsute man with Mediterranean features and a face that seemed to naturally accommodate a permanent grin. When he spotted his wife he hitched a small boy of about two or three years old onto his hip and waved, gesturing with his free hand in a form of sign language that Teresa seemed to understand perfectly.

She glanced at Joanna.

'He wants me to take over with the littlies. Vince has time trials in ten minutes and Rick wants to watch.'

'Vince?'

Teresa pointed to a sullen adolescent sitting on the edge of the 'big kids'' pool, making no attempt to disguise his preoccupation with two giggling teenage girls.

'I know. It's hard to believe he turned twelve last birthday and started high school this year.' She took a sighing breath. 'And of course our youngest was born…er—'

'That's right, you'd just found out you were pregnant—'

'And I'd vowed to stop at three. I blamed Rick for not having the snip.'

Joanna laughed. It was just like old times. But before she had a chance to get maudlin, Teresa began peeling off her clothes. She hesitated a moment, as if she was gauging Joanna's mood, then she broke into a grin as broad as her husband's.

'Last one in's a rotten tomato.'

It didn't take Joanna long to be swept up in the moment and she wondered why she hadn't had the courage to venture to the pool before today. The combination of water, happy, energetic children and lots of noise was a potent enough antidote to the blues to be packaged and sold. She whipped off her shirt, stumbled out of her shorts and, ignoring her friend, plunged into the shallow water. It was truly therapeutic. When she surfaced for air she suddenly found herself in possession of a small child thrust at her by a large man who was making a hasty retreat. Teresa splashed up to her.

'Rick must remember you too.'

'He hasn't changed.'

'Hasn't he? He frets about losing his hair and finding a belly, like most men his age.'

The squirming child was trying to jump out of Joanna's arms onto a large, inflatable floating island. She let him go but before she could take a breath he had taken a flying leap back into her arms.

'That's Carlo. The spoilt baby of the family. As you've probably guessed.'

'He's delightful.' Joanna pulled a silly face and the child laughed before leaping from her arms again.

'Mmm… But a handful.' She grinned. 'If you want a break or actually want to seriously swim, just say the word.'

'I'm fine.' In fact, she hadn't enjoyed herself so much in longer than she could remember and spent the next twenty minutes doing a workout more strenuous than the most vigorous aqua-aerobics class.

Finally Teresa indicated she'd had enough. She glanced at the large clock suspended from the wall.

'I promised I'd watch at least part of Vince's trials and Angie is trying out for the intermediate squad so I might have to leave you to it.' She hesitated. 'Unless you want to come and watch too.'

Joanna was grateful Teresa had the sensitivity to realise she needed a little more time to be able to revisit an activity that she'd never done alone. Watching the Seals was part of her old life, a life that had included Sam and Richard. She vowed she would do it, but not tonight.

'No, thanks. But I hope to come back regularly.'

'Great, we'll look forward to seeing you.'

Joanna watched Teresa gather up the younger two of her brood and corral them into the supervised play area near the kiosk. She sighed and suddenly felt exhausted as she paddled to the side of the pool. It was definitely time to go home.

She glanced across to the adult pool, and noted how busy it was. Maybe next time she'd come straight from work or possibly on her days off and do some laps.

Then she saw him, hoisting himself out of the pool. The most obvious thing about him was his creamy white skin; skin that hadn't been exposed to the boundless Australian summer sun. But he had the same muscular torso, the same firm thighs, the same broad swimmer's shoulders, glistening and rippling. The sight of him, as close to naked as she was likely to see him, took her breath away.

She felt her own near-naked body react with alarming speed and intensity.

He still had the ability to do that to her!

She looked for a means of escape because he mustn't see her like this.

But she was too late.

He was looking directly at her and had an expression on his face that mirrored exactly how she felt. Uncomfortable was putting it mildly.

And now he was walking towards her.

'Joanna!' Richard was smiling but Joanna could tell it was forced. 'Fancy seeing you here. What an amazing coincidence.'

He seemed to be waiting for a reply but she could think of nothing to say. Her thoughts had suddenly entered lockdown mode but her silence didn't put him off.

'I suppose you come here often?'

He was standing uncomfortably close to her. Aware of every gleaming muscle of his body, it took a supreme effort to stop taking in its glory with a full body appraisal. She concentrated on fixing her eyes above shoulder level.

'No, it's the first time...' The words stuck in her throat for the second time that evening and she couldn't bring herself to finish the sentence. The look in his eyes softened. She wished he wasn't so finely tuned in to her emotions.

'I know,' he said. 'Seeing all these kids, the Seals—' As if on cue he was interrupted by a loud whistle coming from where she assumed training of the aspiring young competitors was taking place.

Joanna self-consciously shifted from one foot to the other not quite knowing how to extricate herself from an extremely uncomfortable situation. She was still in her costume and was aware the flimsy, time-worn Lycra did little to conceal every bump and bulge of her out-of-shape body. She wanted to get to the showers, change and go home. She cleared her throat before voicing her thoughts.

'I'm heading off to change and then going home,' she said.

He reached out to touch her arm, probably merely a gesture of friendship or uncomplicated comfort, but she pulled away.

'Can I buy you a cup of tea before you go? Or a cappuccino, if you'd prefer? I noticed the coffee shop on the mezzanine next to the gym is still there and they used to do a reasonable brew.'

His expression was a cross between little-boy pleading and fully-grown-man insistence and she couldn't think of any reasonable excuse to refuse. The thought of a lovely strong cup of tea had its attraction too.

'Okay, but I'm on an early tomorrow and I was hoping to get away soon.'

The twinkle in his lively blue eyes lasted a short second but there was no mistaking what he was thinking. She knew he was a gentleman and wouldn't act on his thoughts. Most women wouldn't have even noticed but she was so tuned to his body language, even now, after more than three years. Joanna took her towel from her shoulders and fixed it around her waist.

'Great. My things are over there on the seat. I won't be a minute.'

She stood at the side of the pool and watched him walk over to the benches. His trunks were still wet and clung to his perfect buttocks like a second skin. An image of a similar front-on view flashed into her mind. To her bewilderment, heat suffused her face and her body responded in a way that brought back downright sexy memories of a time in her life she'd believed she would never revisit. She was definitely glad Richard had his back to her.

This wasn't supposed to happen.

She was over this man and finally getting a divorce was well overdue. She had nothing to give him. Most of her love had dried up and what she had left she gave to the kids she cared for on Matilda. She knew Richard well enough to realise that children were a very important part of a marriage for him. And she didn't have the physical or emotional strength to go through the traumas of IVF, with no guarantees of success.

She banished any romantic thoughts of her husband from her mind.

'A quick cuppa, inconsequential small talk, and then home,' she muttered, wishing she'd had the assertiveness to say no to Richard's invitation in the first place.

Richard was ambling back looking as relaxed as a med student who'd just finished his final exams. He'd pulled on his T-shirt but it stuck to his damp skin and did little to hide the muscles beneath. She thought of her own exposed state, well aware that unlined wet Lycra probably made her look like she was trying out for a wet T-shirt competition. She doubted Richard would have more than a passing interest in her less than perfect body, though.

As if he was reading her mind, he said, 'If you want to change, I can meet you up at the coffee shop.'

'Yes, good idea,' she said, grateful for the opportunity to have a few minutes on her own in close proximity to a mirror. She cringed at the thought of what she looked like—shorn scalp with a double layer of transparent adhesive dressing pasted onto the back of her head, which was still decorated with a small wound and a large multicoloured bruise; a five-year-old swimsuit that only still fitted her because it had lost much of its elasticity with age; and a body that had folds and bulges she'd rather not think about and had also lost much of its elasticity with age...and pregnancy...and lack of time or motivation to keep in shape.

She had to admit she hadn't paid much attention to her appearance over the past few years—she'd had no need. Her *kids* didn't care what she looked like. They hadn't reached the age where the buzz words when it came to the opposite sex were that looking good was all that mattered. She rarely went out socially and if a male paid any attention to her she always managed to put them off in the first five minutes.

So why was what she looked like suddenly so important?

Of course she knew the answer.

She didn't want Richard to think she'd let herself go. Being attractive for *him* was suddenly taking on an importance that made her feel anxious and she certainly didn't need any more stress in her life.

Get a grip of yourself.

She was above all that flirty, sexy, look-at-me stuff that some women seemed to make a vocation of. If it mattered to Richard what she looked like, which she doubted, then he'd changed and it was another reason to get the divorce through as soon as they could.

When she reached the change rooms she untucked her towel from around her waist, dried herself and slipped off her bathers, deciding to leave her shower until she got home. She took care not to look in the direction of the mirrors, which seemed to have multiplied since she'd entered the room. She slipped on her knickers, shorts and T-shirt and finally glanced at the mirror as she attempted to finger-comb her hair.

Whoops!

What hair? She still hadn't gotten used to the bald look.

She took the opportunity to do a full body assessment and decided she had definitely had bad hair days when she'd looked a lot worse.

Taking a deep breath, she gathered her things and headed off to the coffee shop to find Richard.

Richard decided if he couldn't avoid seeing Joanna, he'd make the most of their meeting. A cup of tea had seemed a good idea at the time. Neutral territory, the distraction of others as insurance against awkwardness, a view of the pool area.

His gaze settled on the splashing, yelling, exuberant clump of children in the water.

Happy children.

Healthy children.

Children who had their whole lives ahead of them.

He thought he'd prepared himself for the inevitable memories but the heart-rending emotion he felt took him by surprise. Maybe seeing all the kids either playing or seriously swimming wasn't such a good idea. He'd just have to wait and see.

He found a table that wasn't right on the edge of the mezzanine floor but close enough to get a good view of the pools. His attention drifted to the play pool and he recalled the many evenings he'd spent with Sam and Joanna. Sometimes, like now, he'd been content to just sit and watch the antics of the children and their parents. The youngsters were usually accompanying older sibs who were having more formal lessons and the thing he loved so much about watching them was their lack of inhibition. They were exuberantly happy most of the time but occasionally there'd be a disagreement about someone going ahead of their turn on the slide, or pinching another kid's beach ball. Simple things that usually resulted in all hell letting loose.

But, at times, the parents were even more entertaining. Over the years of taking Sam to the pool and the beach he'd worked out there were three broad groups of parents. First there were the blustery, sergeant-major types—shouting orders no one took any notice of, trying to organise team games that were totally inappropriate for pre-school-aged children, and when the screaming started the aim of this type of parent was to yell at least twice as loud as the child or children to drown them out. Usually the pool attendant had to intervene by asking the parent to leave.

Second was the I-don't-want-to-be-here parent. They would sit on the benches, reading magazines, occasionally glancing up to make sure their child hadn't drowned but otherwise leaving the hapless youngster to their own devices. The poor kid was usually decked out in such an elaborate array of floating devices that he or she could hardly move, let alone protest, and if the child became involved in a mêlée the parent would intentionally ignore the fact their son or daughter was involved and leave someone else to sort it out.

And the third type of parent was…Joanna. Well, she was a perfect example. She came into the pool with a smile on her face that said she was glad to be alive and even more over-joyed to have a beautiful, happy, healthy child to share that joy. She was capable of totally shedding her inhibitions and *playing*, in the fullest sense of the word. That meant blow-ing disgustingly loud raspberries, splashing great spurts of water, not only at the kids but at often bewildered parents, throwing children high in the air, sorting out disagreements by distractions that always left both the aggressors and vic-tims laughing.

He'd seen that natural love of the simple things in life when he'd observed Joanna playing with the toddlers on Matilda Ward. It cut a hole in his heart. Why had someone who loved children so much, who had such a natural affinity for nurtur-ing and mothering, been deprived so cruelly?

He had spent many hours ruminating over this question during the course of Sam's illness but he still hadn't come up with an answer.

It was meant to be?

Every cloud has a silver lining?

What goes around comes around?

All glib clichés that lost their relevance in the brutal real-ity of life, he thought.

Joanna…

He watched her climb the stairs and wondered if he was falling in love with her all over again, for different, more en-during reasons.

There was no doubt she was still the full package in the looks department. He loved her new curves that she'd displayed so tantalisingly in that gorgeous almost see-through costume. The naked-but-not-quite-naked look had blood coursing through his veins at a speed he definitely wasn't used to. And not only was her body different but she was happy again.

She'd been stick thin and gaunt when he'd left to go overseas and she'd rarely smiled. Her GP had diagnosed depression and done all the right things. Referred her for grief counselling, suggested a support group and prescribed an antidepressant. But she'd not followed through with his recommendations and said she would get through in her own way and her own time. He'd felt so guilty when he'd left but Joanna had made it quite clear that his presence in her life was making her recovery more difficult. Her telling him that, over and over, had been like a series of body blows but it had probably been her way of trying to spare him the pain of experiencing her suffering.

No wonder she didn't want to get close to him again.

Her new life seemed to have left the past where it belonged. And good for her.

But—there was no other way of saying it—his heart still ached for her and he still wanted to be the one to be there for her, her significant other.

She stood at the top of the stairs, gazing around the shop, looking for him.

He waved and she manoeuvred her way through the scattered tables to where he sat.

'Hi, sit down. I haven't ordered yet. What would you like?'

'A white tea, thanks.'

'That's all? Nothing to eat?'

'No, thanks, just the tea.'

They were carrying on a conversation like wary strangers. Richard got up to get the drinks and came back with a packet of sandwiches and Joanna's favourite chocolate bar. He smiled sheepishly, expecting to be reprimanded.

'They had a special on chocolate and I thought we deserved an indulgence as a reward for our hard work in the pool.'

It was worth the risk—she actually rewarded him for his humour with a smile.

'I don't know whether I deserve any. I spent the best part of an hour playing with Teresa Deleo's youngest. Do you remember the Deleos?'

'How could I forget? If you dared to cheer louder than— was his name Rick?' Joanna nodded. 'For a child that wasn't his you'd risk life and limb.'

Joanna laughed and it was like the winter sun emerging from behind a dark cloud and lighting up the whole world with happiness. For a moment he was lost for words and just wanted to soak in the warmth of her.

'That's right. Do you remember Teresa was pregnant?'

'Not really. Men don't take much notice. That's my excuse, anyway.'

'You're forgiven. She was only a couple of months, I think. Their fourth. Little Carlo, the baby I had the pleasure of borrowing to play with, well, he's the result.'

Richard looked at Joanna for a moment, trying to gauge if there were any regrets, any resentment that she didn't have a child of her own. For a change, her face was open and easy to read. She had enjoyed her time with her friend's child and unless she hid it well, she had no bad feelings.

'You probably had a harder workout than me. You definitely deserve chocolate.'

She took the offered chocolate and carefully unwrapped it to expose a couple of triangles, which she snapped off, offering one to him.

'No, thanks, I'll start on the sandwiches.'

For some reason he expected she'd refuse the food and he

interpreted her acceptance as a symbol of her acceptance of him. Not as a husband or potential lover but someone she was comfortable sitting with in a coffee shop, simply sharing a hot drink.

It was a start, if only a small step, and would make their work together easier.

He opened the sandwiches and offered the package to her but she shook her head, already sucking the chocolate, making it last as she always had.

They ate and drank in silence for a couple of minutes. Richard wanted to ask her so many questions, personal questions like what had finally brought her out of her depression? Had it been a difficult decision to embark on nursing children with cancer? How did she cope on her own? Did she still sing? *Had she had any lovers?*

But it was too soon and she would probably think it was none of his business, so instead they talked about work and a little about his trip overseas and nothing about what really mattered. There was a film of tension hanging between them that they were both trying their hardest to pretend didn't exist.

When they finished it was close to nine-thirty, half an hour before the centre's closing time, and the staff of the coffee shop made it clear they were keen for their remaining customers to leave so they could get on with the cleaning up.

'Do you want a lift home?' Richard offered. He didn't know if she had a car.

'No, thanks, I've brought my car.'

'I'll walk you out to the car park, then.'

She shrugged as if she didn't have the energy to resist and he followed her down the stairs. They walked past the main pool in silence. The Seal Squad had disbanded and gone home and there were only a few stragglers in the play pool—certainly no sign of the Deleos, to Richard's relief.

'You don't have to walk me to the car,' Joanna said when they reached the foyer. 'It's just over there.'

He looked in the direction she was pointing and squinted at the few vehicles remaining in the car park.

'The truck or the hatchback? My guess is the truck.'

She laughed. 'Guess again.'

'Well, if it's the hatchback, it looks suspiciously like a limited model. Never mind the gentlemanly valour, my motive is to check out your wheels.'

She'd replaced the large family wagon she'd had when he'd left. The smaller car would be much more practical and the small but sporty model suited her perfectly. To his relief she didn't protest when he began to walk with her towards her car and when they got there she turned and hesitated.

'I'm glad I came tonight,' she said in a voice that trembled slightly.

'So am I. Maybe it's something we can do again?'

'Maybe.'

It was a *maybe* smile that hinted at possibilities, combined with the old sparkle in her eyes that he remembered so well, that suggested... He couldn't resist. He'd just have to find out.

He touched her lips with his fingertips—simply to give her the opportunity to refuse—before he kissed her.

But she didn't refuse.

The taste of her lips was a tantalising rediscovery of a sweet and tender place he'd thought he'd never experience again. Her skin was soft as fine oriental silk, her breath warm and laced with the slight scent of chocolate and Earl Grey tea. She exuded sensuality from every pore and he was certain she knew what effect she was having on his self-control. He couldn't stop.

He nibbled her lower lip and then teased her perfect teeth with his tongue until she opened up to him.

Her eyes were seductively closed and the corner of her left

upper lid twitched slightly. She held her breath while he deepened his kiss and their bodies pressed so close, Richard could feel the fluttering of her heart and the faintest whole-body tremble that set his own muscles into a state of tension that could only be relieved in one way. His hands moved slickly down from to her shoulders to her back and then to her softly rounded buttocks.

He wanted her so much but he felt her tense as if she'd read his mind. Her eyes snapped open to reveal a dark, agitated sea of uncertainty. She pulled away and took a sharp breath.

'I can't do this, Richard. I'm sorry but you shouldn't even expect me to try. There's too much at stake. You don't know me any more. I don't know you...'

She fumbled for her keys and opened her car door.

'I...I shouldn't have...' Richard couldn't find the words to express how he felt.

Already in the driver's seat, Joanna looked close to tears and he couldn't think of anything he could do or say to reassure her, to explain his impulsive actions.

'Neither should I. Goodbye, Richard.' Her voice was now as hard as steel, emotionless, painfully like the many times when she'd closed off the part of herself he'd so much wanted to reach, to comfort, to *heal*.

She was right. It had been a mistake.

'Goodbye Jo,' he whispered, but she already had the engine running and, with a squeal of rubber on bitumen, drove away into the night.

CHAPTER SIX

Over the next week both Joanna and Richard made a very good job of ignoring what had happened in the car park of the local leisure centre on Monday night. No one would ever suspect there was anything more to their relationship than that between consultant and dedicated nurse. When Friday came, Richard bowed out of band practice and was glad he was on call the whole weekend. Fortunately he had enough to keep him busy to take his mind off thinking about his wife, who he understood was about to start working nights the following Wednesday after two days off. Though he'd miss her on the ward they wouldn't have to keep up the pretence that their relationship was purely a professional one.

The fortnightly multi-disciplinary team meeting finished at about eleven and when Richard came into the ward, he didn't expect to see Joanna. It was her day off. She was in the chemo suite with Danny Sims and his father, Lynne, Tracey, Kerry, half a dozen kids who were well enough to move from their beds and a very tall young man Richard didn't recognise—who seemed to be the centre of their adoring attention. Richard poked his head in the door to say hello before he began his official rounds. He was curious to know what was going on.

'Hi, Danny.' He acknowledged the boy who was having his second chemo session and looked remarkably relaxed and comfortable, considering the high doses of medication being delivered.

'Hi, Doc Howell.' He raised his hand in greeting and smiled as if it was his lucky day. 'You'll never guess who's here.'

'Someone pretty special?' Richard said. The boy's delight was written all over his face.

Danny chuckled. 'You're not wrong.'

The towering young visitor turned and grinned. He was wearing a polo shirt with the state basketball team logo on the pocket but Richard had no clue as to his identity. He didn't follow the sport and the fact that he'd been away meant he'd lost touch with a lot of the local news.

'Hi, I'm Bobby Masters.' He paused as if waiting for signs of recognition.

Richard offered his hand and Bobby shook it vigorously. 'I'm Dr Howell, Danny's doctor.'

The excited chatter that had filled the room a few moments ago suddenly stilled as if waiting for Richard's acknowledgement of the obvious celebrity status of Bobby Masters. Richard wondered if he should admit he had no idea who he was or alternatively make a polite excuse and leave. He was rescued from his dilemma by Joanna, who was smiling broadly. She reached for Danny's hand and gave it a squeeze.

'It's not every day you get to meet the captain of the Western Slammers, let alone be presented with a team jersey signed by all the players in last year's premiership side.'

The uninhibited rapture on Danny's face was impossible to ignore and his joy was contagious. He held up the basketball uniform covered in signatures and a photograph of Bobby, also signed.

'Wow, I'm impressed.' Though he didn't share the boy's obvious love of the sport, Richard *was* genuinely impressed.

'It's a privilege to meet you Bobby. And you've undoubtedly made young Danny's day,' Richard added, directing his comments to the basketball player.

'I reckon he deserves a bit of special attention.' Bobby then glanced at Joanna with a mix of admiration and youthful respect. 'But it wouldn't have happened without Joanna's...er... Well, let's say she can be extremely persuasive. She organised the whole thing.'

Joanna laughed. 'Just doing my job.'

At that moment a photographer appeared in the doorway and Richard took the opportunity to make his excuses and leave.

'I have to go now, Danny, but I'll see you later to check how you're going.'

'Thanks, Dr Howell.' It was Danny's father who spoke. 'Thanks for everything.' He shifted his gaze to Joanna and looked on the verge of tears.

Richard nodded and slipped quietly out of the room.

Half an hour later he bumped into Joanna coming from the direction of the chemo suite, which was now quiet. The photo session had finished and the celebrity guest appeared to have left.

'You knew this was happening?' He directed his question to Joanna.

Danny's father popped his head out of the parents' room with a bottle of juice in his hand.

'I heard a rumour she organised the whole thing,' Danny's father said, with a broad grin, rivalling his son's recent rapt expression.

'Really?'

Joanna seemed to have an endless supply of generosity and goodwill when it came to looking after her young patients, which extended beyond her usual working hours. She answered him with a wink, not appearing to want any recognition or praise.

For the rest of the week he missed having her around on the ward and it was obvious other staff did as well without actually saying so. He'd hear them talk about her and leave messages in the notes for the night staff that were obviously meant for Joanna.

If he was early enough to catch her before her shift finished he found himself confiding in her about the day-to-day events on the ward. She missed a lot of the bread-and-butter happenings that were taken for granted by the staff working day shifts and seemed to relish information about things like how Rebecca's dance classes were going or what Liam's reaction was to having his whole year-two class come in for his birthday party.

There weren't enough hours in the day, Richard mused, and the thought occurred to him that the time he valued the most was the time he spent with Joanna.

'Come in, Richard. It's great to see you again. I heard you were coming back to our fair city but I wasn't sure when.' Adam Segal extended his lightly tanned, freshly manicured hand in greeting.

Richard hadn't been able to find any credible reason to procrastinate in initiating divorce proceedings and had made the appointment with his solicitor for late afternoon on his one half-day off for the week. It didn't seem right, though, and more than once he'd considered cancelling the appointment and came close to missing it that afternoon.

He arrived just in time.

Though he considered himself an optimist, on days like today he believed there was a lot of truth in Murphy's Law. He'd predictably got caught up with work, having to deal with Liz and Phillip Bryant whose two-year-old daughter had finally been scheduled for surgery. She was to have the tumour, which was rapidly filling her abdominal cavity, removed the following day and he'd ordered a transfusion to boost her low red cells prior to her operation. Unfortunately she'd had a rare, unexpected reaction to the blood and had slipped into severe respiratory distress.

The crisis had been treated and her condition stabilised in the few short hours after her transfer to the intensive care unit but the drama had tipped the balance of Liz Bryant's already fragile mental state into what could be loosely described as borderline hysteria. He'd managed to calm her down but it had taken up most of his afternoon and the last thing he felt like doing was starting the onerous process of filing for divorce.

But it had to be done.

It wasn't fair on Joanna to delay any longer. She'd worked so hard to make a new life, she deserved to be free.

'Hello, Adam. It's good to see you again too.'

'Come through into my office.'

Richard followed the solicitor down a short corridor and into a spacious, tastefully decorated room with a huge window looking out on the Swan River.

Richard sat down on a leather-upholstered club chair while Adam Segal settled behind a highly polished, antique oak desk. He opened his laptop, pressed a few keys and then focused his attention on his client.

'So what brings you here? What can I do for you?'

Richard realised the best thing to do was get straight to the point.

'I want to divorce Jo.'

The elevation of the lawyer's brows was so slight Richard wondered if he'd imagined it, but realised it was part of the man's job to have the ability to turn body language on and off at will. He wrote something down in a ring-bound file and then looked up with the hint of a sympathetic smile on his face.

'You know my area of expertise is company law and financial advice, not family law.'

'Yes. I'm aware of that but I'd prefer if you could handle it.'

He'd known Adam for many years. They'd gone to uni together and Adam had met Joanna socially several times. He knew that shouldn't make any difference, but it did. It somehow made what he imagined would be a brutally impersonal procedure a little more tolerable.

'Mmm…' Adam rubbed his clean-shaven chin thoughtfully. 'I'd be happy to guide you through the process if it's clear cut. Are there any possible complications? Custody issues? Property issues where there might be some dispute?'

'No. No children and we sold the house not long after I left for the U.K. Joanna has her own, smaller home now and I agreed that she could do whatever she wanted with the proceeds of the sale of the Barclay Street place.'

The eyebrows definitely went up this time.

'Generous,' he said, and wrote some more in his file. 'As this is obviously all new to you I'll give you the family court booklet to read and the application papers. When you've been through those I'll see you again and we can complete the application and organise to serve the notice on your wife. After that it's relatively simple.'

Adam picked up the phone and pressed one of the buttons.

'Could you ask Marie if she can get me the divorce application paperwork and then bring it in?' He looked up apologetically. 'You understand this isn't my usual field.'

Richard felt a little guilty but then remembered his friend had never been shy of charging hefty fees.

'Thanks, Adam, I appreciate it.'

The meeting was effectively wound up when the receptionist, who had taken his details when he'd arrived, came in with a folder. The lawyer handed them over after doing a quick check of the contents.

'Perhaps you could make an appointment in about a week.' He hesitated. 'And I'm so sorry to hear about you and Joanna.'

I'm sorry too, Richard thought as he stood up and shook his friend's hand.

'I'll make an appointment when I check my schedule for next week.'

When Richard arrived home, he felt exhausted. He discarded the folder Adam had given him, vowing he would go through it on the weekend and make another appointment after that, without delay. He had the feeling the longer he postponed the process of actually signing the papers that finally struck the death knell for his marriage, the less likely he would go through with it.

But it was what Joanna wanted. She'd made that perfectly clear and he had no valid reason to persuade her to try again… other than that he still loved her. He knew that for certain now. Yes, she'd changed and she'd made a new life for herself but, in a peculiar way, her newfound independence endeared her to him even more. Any doubts he'd had while he'd been overseas had vanished after the first conversation they'd had together. The problem was, he could never tell her because she didn't need the added complication of dealing with his futile emotions.

The rest of the evening dragged painfully slowly and when he was just about to go to bed his phone rang. He glanced at the small screen on his cellphone and recognised the number of Lady Lawler.

'Hello, Richard Howell,' he said, now fully alert and wondering why the hospital was contacting him. He wasn't on call.

'Hi, Dr Howell. It's Barbara, charge nurse on Matilda Ward. I hope you don't mind me ringing.'

'Of course not. A problem with one of our patients?'

'Er...' The nurse hesitated and then cleared her throat. 'Not exactly. I just wanted to have a quick word with you about Joanna Raven.'

'Joanna?' His heart rate quickened and he swallowed the lump that had suddenly formed in his throat. Why on earth would she want to talk to him about Jo? At ten-thirty at night. Had something happened to her?

'Yes. I may be concerned unnecessarily but she spent over an hour this evening talking to Danny Sims's mother on the phone. When she finally finished, Jo seemed close to tears and without any explanation she took off for about fifteen minutes. She's never done anything like that before and if I stuck strictly to staff protocols I should report the incident to the director of nursing.'

'That seems harsh.'

'I know, and when she came back she was fine, perfectly composed. I just thought you should know and maybe have a word with her, if you have a moment. You've spent a lot of time with the Sims family and know them better than anyone. You and Jo seem to get on really well together as well. I know she holds you in high regard. She refused to admit anything was wrong to me. Said she just needed to go to the toilet in a hurry, but I've known her long enough to suspect there's more to it than that. In fact, she's been a bit edgy all week.'

'Okay, I'll speak to her tomorrow. Her shift finishes at seven?'

'That's right.'

'So she'll probably want to get some sleep during the day.' Much as he would have liked to jump in his car and drive to the hospital straight away, he realised he was overreacting. He'd try and call her some time during the following afternoon. 'I'll certainly have a quiet word with her tomorrow, if I can.'

'Thanks Dr Howell. I wasn't sure what else to do.'

'You did the right thing to ring me.'

Richard spent a restless night, drifting in and out of sleep in between thinking of Joanna and speculating about what it was concerning the Sims family that had upset her. If it was because Danny had the same tumour that had taken the life of their son he definitely needed to discuss the problem with her on a professional as well as a personal level.

The last time he looked at his bedside clock it was 5:00 a.m. and, after what only seemed like a few moments, the buzz of his alarm jolted him out of his slumbers.

The beginning of another day.

Despite the fact Joanna was so tired she could hardly put one foot in front of the other, she couldn't get to sleep. First, it was an uncomfortably humid day and a lukewarm shower did little to either cool her down or refresh her. Second, she seemed hyper-alert to every sound in her usually quiet neighbourhood that morning. First it was the garbage truck, then a mob of raucous laughing kookaburras and she finally gave up when the noise of chainsaws pruning street trees started at about eight-thirty. And, of course, this was all superimposed on the underlying unsettled feeling she'd had since Jenny Sims had phoned and asked her if she could explain some of the things she and her husband didn't understand about Danny's illness, including his prognosis.

Of course her answer had been that they should discuss any queries they had with the doctor, but then Jenny, with Pete in the background, had launched into a heart-wrenching account of how they blamed themselves for their son's illness. They should have known something was wrong when Danny had developed back pain after the school athletics carnival;

they'd ignored the fact that he'd complained of tiredness, thinking it was purely due to a growth spurt and starting at a new school; when he'd seemed to lose his usually voracious appetite they'd assumed he was pigging out on junk food after school. Jenny also felt guilty about commencing full-time work at the beginning of the year when Danny had started high school, and they both believed their GP had waited too long before ordering X-rays.

Joanna had listened with the kind of understanding that came from having been in that same dark whirlpool of guilt, regret and blame. She knew the agony of going over and over in her mind what she hadn't done and not knowing whether it would have made any difference. She'd suffered the despair of a depression she couldn't shake when she'd realised Sam wouldn't survive. And she'd rejected her husband when he had tried so desperately to help her and had probably needed her more than she'd needed him.

Of course, she hadn't voiced any of her thoughts to the Simses but hoped just letting them express their concerns and pointing out they didn't have to shoulder the burden alone would help. They'd thanked her and seemed calmer when she'd hung up but it had taken its toll on her own peace of mind. She'd managed to hold herself together until she finally excused herself and finished the call.

Then she'd had to escape. It had only taken five therapeutic minutes in the nurses' locker room for the tears to wash away at least some of the anguish of her memories. They'd been so vivid. She'd thought time had done its healing work but she'd been wrong. Thankfully she'd had the distraction of work to get her through the long night and she'd managed to fob off Barbara's concerned enquiries about her wellbeing.

She was glad she had the weekend off—her next shift was Monday night—so if she didn't get any sleep that day she could always catch up on her days off.

After a light breakfast, a banana smoothie, and a tidy up of her house she finally drifted off to sleep at about lunch-time. She'd turned her phone off and hung the 'Quiet, Shift Worker Sleeping' sign on her front door and woke six hours later feeling refreshed…and restless. Usually she was quite content with her own company and had got used to living alone, but tonight she felt she needed people around her.

She looked at her watch and it was just after six. She had plenty of time to have a shower, a bite to eat and make it to choir practice with time to spare.

Richard called Joanna's number several times that afternoon but had been diverted to her message bank each time. He'd left several messages for her to contact him but, at five-thirty in the afternoon, she still hadn't got back to him.

He refused to imagine the worst. She was probably just sleeping. Although it had been a long time in the past, he still recalled how exhausting working nights could be. He made up his mind to call around to see her the following day if she still wasn't answering her phone and decided not to resist James Francis's pleas to make up the numbers at band prac-tice that evening. It would take his mind off Joanna. Or that was the plan.

He drove the short distance to his house, microwaved a plate of yesterday's leftover ravioli and sat in his living room, eating his meal while watching the evening news. When he finished, leaving half the soggy remains of the pasta, he show-ered and changed into casual clothes, gathered his saxophone case and walked back to the hospital.

When he arrived he was greeted by the dozen or so mem-bers of the band as if he was a celebrity and he not only en-joyed playing in the band, but the time passed quickly.

'See you next week,' was the farewell comment from James.

'Yes, I'll try and make it,' he said, being careful not to commit himself. Unexpected demands often came up that he couldn't avoid and he had a clinical heads of department meeting the following Friday afternoon that he'd been told might continue into the early evening.

He strode out of the lecture theatre and set off along the walkway with a much lighter heart than when he'd arrived. Deep in thought in an endeavour to plan the best use of his time off on the weekend, he rounded a corner and nearly collided with...

'Joanna? Is that you?'

The question was redundant. He could easily tell who it was. She was wearing snug-fitting white cropped pants that accentuated the golden colour of her calves, topped by a sleeveless T-shirt with a scoop neck that revealed a glimpse of gorgeous cleavage. A white-peaked, Oliver Twist style cap shaded her eyes from the glow of the lamps that illuminated the path and made it impossible to assess her mood from the expression on her face.

She hesitated as if in some kind of dilemma about how to answer him.

'Are you all right?' he added as she lifted her head. Her eyes connected with his and now he could see she was annoyed.

'Why shouldn't I be?' Her tone wasn't exactly hostile but she obviously wasn't pleased to see him.

'Er...' How could he tactfully broach the fact that Barbara had been worried about her and asked him if he would follow up her concerns? Maybe the best tactic would be the truth. He'd never been good at hedging around issues. 'I wanted to talk to you, and planned to call around and see you tomorrow.'

Her eyes narrowed.

'About the divorce?'

In all honesty he'd managed to put all thoughts of the divorce to the back of his mind and hadn't yet made a follow-up appointment to see his lawyer friend.

'No, something else.' The static weight of his saxophone case was beginning to make his arm ache so he placed it on the paving between his feet. The diversion also served the purpose of giving him another couple of moments to decide what he was going to say. A young couple with a small child in tow walked past and looked at them curiously. It wasn't the best place for a gently probing conversation about issues that were close to both their hearts.

'It's a delicate matter,' he continued. 'And maybe we could go somewhere more private.'

Her brow furrowed in a frown.

'Where?'

'Are you walking?'

'Yes.'

'Can I walk with you? My place is in the same direction and maybe—'

'Okay. I'd rather we go back to *my* place, have a cuppa, if it's so important—this delicate matter.'

Richard sighed with relief. He'd been expecting the third degree.

'Yes. That would be perfect. It shouldn't take long. When's your next shift at the hospital?'

'I have the weekend and go back Monday night. I'll probably be awake most of the night because I slept this afternoon. That's the trouble with working nights, you have a couple of days off to get back into your normal diurnal rhythm and then it starts all over again.'

They talked little on the brief walk to Joanna's and the limited conversation they had was superficial small talk. Richard recognised the house at the front of the block and followed

Joanna to her place at the back. She opened the sliding door and Richard followed her inside.

'Sit down,' she said, as if she were about to entertain the tax inspector.

He sat on the sofa and watched her walk into the kitchen. Yes, she looked decidedly uncomfortable, which was the last thing he wanted.

'How was choir practice?' The question was merely an extension of the conversation they'd started on the walk home when he'd rambled on about the band and the pieces they were rehearsing. It had simply been a strategy to break the silence.

'Okay.' She turned her back on him and reached up to a cupboard where several mugs were stacked. 'Someone suggested we could look into seeing if any of the kids wanted to be involved.'

'You mean patients?'

She turned to face him. 'And possibly members of their families or friends as well.'

He took a moment to process what she had just told him. Definitely a good idea from the viewpoint of morale but the practicalities of getting a group of sick and injured children together and transporting them to the town hall, the venue that had been booked for the concert, would make the project difficult to say the least.

'How would—?'

Joanna smiled. 'I know what you're going to say. The physical restraints imposed by half the performers being in wheelchairs or hospital beds or hooked up to IVs and various monitors would make a concert in the normal sense impossible.'

She had his curiosity aroused.

'Tea or coffee?' she asked as she turned off the bubbling kettle.

'Tea, thanks.'

She poured the drinks and brought them over to the low table near where he sat. Also on the tray was a small plate of home-made coconut slice, one of his favourites. He thought how touching it would be if Jo had made them especially for him, but of course she'd had no idea he was going to visit. As if reading his mind, she picked up the plate and offered him a piece. He took a bite.

'This is even better than I remember.'

Removing the tea bag, she stirred milk into her tea.

'It's probably my downfall. I still love baking.' She cast her eyes downwards. 'Although it's not the same…' Her voice trailed off.

'Delicious,' he said. 'I'm glad you still like to cook.'

He suddenly realised what a tactless thing that had been to say. He leaving her was no reason to stop cooking the things he'd always liked. In fact, talking to Joanna felt like walking on thin ice. He had no idea where the fragile areas lay and certainly didn't want a dunking. How much of the past was out of bounds?

'What were you saying about the concert?' Talking about the present was a much safer bet.

She leaned back in her chair and rested her tea on her knee, taking a measured breath.

'Well, if you're really interested…'

'I am. After all, I've been persuaded to perform so my reputation's at stake.'

She smiled. Richard was relieved she still showed traces of the sense of humour that he'd thought she'd lost.

'One of the nurses on General Surgical—I don't think you know her, Lorraine Henderson…' He shook his head and she continued. 'Her husband is a professional video photographer, does wedding DVDs and the like.' She took another breath and it was evident by the look on her face she was discussing the beginnings of an idea she was already passionate about. He let her go on without interruption. 'To cut a long story short, the whole concept is to create a movie of the kids without having to necessarily move them from their beds, let alone the hospital.'

She was beaming now, expectantly waiting for his comment. He certainly didn't want to put a damper on the suggestion before it had gone past the planning stage but he had his doubts.

'Sounds fabulous. Definitely original.' He hesitated a moment. 'Have you got a big enough pool of talent?'

Her eyes narrowed. She'd undoubtedly interpreted his comment as criticism rather than simple caution.

'You don't think it would work,' she said flatly. All her previous enthusiasm vanished.

'I didn't say that.'

She took another mouthful of tea and brushed some coconut off the table.

'Have another.' She offered him the plate again.

'No, thanks.'

The both sipped their drinks and it suddenly seemed the most difficult task in the world to broach the subject of her talk with Danny Sims's parents. Maybe he would leave it to another day but Joanna solved the dilemma for him.

'So what was so important you'd planned to visit me on my day off to discuss it?'

Right. *She'd* brought up the subject. And it needed to be discussed. He owed it to Barbara to at least try to find out what the problem had been.

'Barbara asked me to talk to you.'

She put her cup on the table and crossed her arms across her chest. He took it as a defensive gesture.

'Barbara? I don't understand. Why would Barb—?'

'She was worried about you.' He leaned across and put his hand on hers, relieved she didn't pull away.

'Worried about what?' He imagined the cogs of her brain turning but he had the feeling she knew what he was talking about.

'She said you were upset last night after talking to the Simses. I can guess at why—'

'You didn't tell her?' Joanna cut in sharply, and Richard felt her tension increase.

'You mean about us and Sam? Of course I didn't. That's our own private business.'

'Yes.' Her eyes connected with his and the look she conveyed was one of understanding, of the bond of a shared past.

'What did Jenny and Pete want to talk about?'

Joanna withdrew her hand and edged away from him. He didn't want her to reject him and he felt partly responsible for any distress she was experiencing. Coming back and opening a window to a time that had been so traumatic for both of them wasn't something he'd planned.

She attempted a smile but it was unconvincing.

'They were suffering from information overload and started asking questions like "What are Danny's chances of pulling through? Will he suffer? What is the success rate of the treatment?"' She sighed. 'All things I'm sure you've told them already but they didn't want to believe the odds are so heavily stacked against their son.'

'And what did you tell them?'

'It's not my role to spout cold statistics. I told them to ask you.' She paused. 'I said you were a wonderful doctor...' she flushed and looked away '...and not to be worried about talking through things with you, no matter how long it takes.'

'And?' He wouldn't let her stop there. Her lower lip began to tremble.

'I said they're going through exactly the same emotions

as just about every other parent of a child who is diagnosed with cancer.'

Richard knew there was more. He hadn't lived with and loved Joanna for over seven years without being able to tune in to her emotions. He didn't want to push her, though. So he waited for her to decide whether she would reveal that little extra. She looked up and her pupils dilated. A single tear escaped and coursed down her cheek. She sniffed.

'They wanted to know if I'd nursed any patients with Ewing's before or if Danny was the first.' Her tormented gaze was again fixed on his as if continuing the conversation was a challenge for her. The look in her eyes said she was determined not to break down. Why? Richard wondered. During the good times they'd had together they'd always been honest with each other, always been able to unburden their worries and share the load. He wanted so much for her to share with him now.

On impulse, without a care for the consequences, he moved to sit next to her. Draping his arm across her shoulders and drawing her towards him seemed a natural thing to do. Again she didn't resist and leaned into his embrace.

'What did you tell them?' he whispered as he reached across and began gently stroking her hair. She sighed and stilled his hand by grasping it with both of hers.

'I said Danny was the first. Which wasn't strictly true. I've seen one other case—a boy called Callum—but his tumour was picked up early and he survived. I didn't want to get their hopes up.' She turned her face to him and for the first time since Richard had been back she dropped her protective shield of guarded coolness and let him close to her.

'Danny reminds you of Sam?' Richard said gently.

'Yes, but Sam was our son and there's a world of difference... He was our son.'

He knew what he wanted to say but the words stuck in his

throat. He wanted to tell Joanna that the pain of losing Sam was the worst thing he had ever experienced; that he'd hid the sadness and guilt because he'd wanted to be strong for his wife and child; that he'd never been able to share the dark depths of his emotions with anyone, not even her.

'You never cried for him.' Joanna looked away and began running her fingers back and forth along the back of his hand with a restlessness he recognised. She was still hiding something. He stilled her hand.

'I never let anyone *see* me cry.'

'But you were always a tower of strength, never lost control.'

And that was exactly what he had wanted her to believe. One of them had had to stay at least outwardly strong, and he'd spent years as a doctor fine-tuning the skill of keeping his distance, of not getting emotionally involved. But if he'd known his intentional coolness would drive a wedge between him and his wife, he would have willingly shared the truth of how devastating that time had been for him. He hadn't wanted to be pitied, though. His job, in some ways, had made it worse. He could recite the statistics, he knew the odds, but he'd prayed every day for a miracle. And deep down he'd assumed he'd failed as both a father and a husband and nursed the irrational belief that he had been somehow to blame.

'It was a facade, Joanna. It was the only way I knew to help you through. I thought—'

'Oh, Richard. Why didn't you tell me? I was convinced you'd stopped caring. That you'd fallen out of love with me and I was a burden to you.'

He released her hand and drew her closer. He gently kissed her forehead as relief flooded his senses like the first rains after a brutal and unforgiving drought.

'I still love you, Joanna.' He could see the beginning of tears brimming in her eyes but he'd come this far and had to tell her. 'After I left to go to the U.K. I tried to stop loving you but...' Words suddenly seemed inadequate. He tilted her chin so he was looking straight into the depths of her dark, unfathomable eyes. 'It might sound like a cliché but there is no other way to tell you.' He attempted to swallow the lump in his throat but it stubbornly stayed put and made his voice rough and erratic. 'The years I shared with you and Sam... They were the best of my life.'

She reached up and placed her hands behind his head. Her touch was an exquisitely sensual caress. He wanted to hold her close in his arms, to rock away the years of hurt and mis-understanding. He wanted to kiss her but the most precious thing for him would be the gift of her love. He realised it was asking too much so soon. He imagined she was more con-fused than him. They had only touched the surface of a past full of misconceptions, misplaced untruths and delusions. Both their lives had changed and they needed to get to know each other all over again.

It was a start.

If Joanna was willing...

'What are you thinking?' she said.

He hesitated but wanted to start afresh and be perfectly honest with her.

'I was thinking how much we've both changed.'

She surprised him with a smile.

'For better or worse?' Joanna asked, but it wasn't a fair question and the answer fitted somewhere in between.

'Neither. Just different.'

'Because it's just you and me? No baby, no child to cement our relationship? You know, for such a long time I thought life would never be normal again. Sam was... Sam was our future...' She took a deep sighing breath. 'He was a gift... and I only had one shot at being a mother. I didn't expect it to be easy but I was prepared to give it my best and I blew it.'

Richard leaned forward and kissed her lightly on the mouth, with what he hoped was tenderness and reassurance. His lips moved to her forehead then her temple. Not only was she attractive on the outside but she had an inner beauty that she guarded like a precious jewel. She had been a wonderful mother and it hurt to hear her say she was to blame.

'You can't mean that.'

'I don't know…no…I didn't mean—' Her eyes were moist and brimming with sadness.

Richard cut short her answer by placing his index finger on her mouth. He felt responsible for the anguish that accompanied their memories. He saw much more hope and joy in looking forward and he desperately wanted Joanna to be part of his future.

'I'm sorry I've made you unhappy. If there's anything I can do…'

She swallowed. The sadness left her eyes and was replaced by a dogged certainty. She'd made up her mind about something—something that had erased the negativity.

'Stay tonight.' The words were barely a whisper. He wondered if he'd heard correctly and battled to contain his surprise. He'd been expecting a rejection.

'Are you sure?'

'I've got nothing to lose, Richard.'

But he knew, in reality, how much they both could lose. Sleeping with Joanna now was a huge gamble but he didn't know how to say no. He wanted her with a powerful passion he'd thought he'd never feel again. He stood up, reached for Joanna's hand and she led him to the bedroom.

CHAPTER SEVEN

To ASK Richard to stay, to share her bed and invite the inevitable consequences, wasn't a snap decision for Joanna. From the day she'd first seen him sitting in the canteen she'd known she still had feelings for him but couldn't even consider acting on them. *She'd* closed herself off from Richard and driven him away three years ago. Even if he forgave her, there was no way things could be the same. A divorce had seemed the logical solution; to cut the one remaining tie they had. She'd worked hard to make a satisfying life that didn't involve Richard. She'd thought his return would bring back the pain of the past. Of course it had, but talking with her husband, the only person who had truly known what her grieving had been like, was a release as well as a comfort.

And she wanted…needed physical comfort, to be cradled in his arms and desired as a sensual, attractive woman. Her mantra echoed in her mind.

I'm a good nurse. I love the children I care for and that's all that matters.

But it wasn't enough, it wasn't all that mattered.

She needed to be loved as well.

Richard had told her he still loved her and she was prepared to take the risk to find out if the sexual spark of their relationship was still alive. The last thing she needed was for Richard to feel sorry for her. In fact, if he'd refused her invitation, that spark would have been extinguished once and for all.

She had nothing to lose, but so much to gain if…

They reached the bedroom door and hesitated before opening it.

'You're beautiful, Joanna,' Richard whispered as he cradled her face with both hands and leaned towards her.

The gentle, familiar touch of his lips on hers was an exquisite pleasure. He lingered, his mouth moving across her upper lip in tender possession. His eyes were open as he deepened his kiss and Joanna felt a swamping, pulsing heat she hadn't felt for a long time. Her heart quickened. She saw Richard's pupils dilate just before she closed her eyes and melted into his embrace.

'Not here.' Richard's husky voice brought her back to reality.

'No,' she said as he opened the door, but they lingered on the threshold as if unsure whether to take the next, life-changing step.

After only a moment's hesitation he drew her towards him, their arms entwined with every point of contact between their bodies alive with vibrant energy.

Joanna could tell Richard felt it too and they were both powerless to resist.

Her hands shook slightly as she began to explore and rediscover Richard's body and she now realised there was no turning back. The sizzle of sexual tension that they both knew was buzzing between them was like static electricity building up in air heavy with anticipation and humidity before a thunderous summer storm.

Her hands seemed to take on a life of their own but it was her mind that savoured every sensual touch. She dragged her fingers down the roughness of Richard's cheeks and then to

his sleek, damp neck. His sweat smelled seductively mascu-
line and she tasted it with the tip of her tongue.

'No,' he groaned, but she knew he meant yes. He guided
her towards the bed and she showed no resistance as his hands
worked their way under her top and up her back until he found
the fastening of her bra. While he skilfully undressed her
he sought out her errant tongue and devoured it. As the kiss
progressed, Joanna felt she was losing herself in something
wonderfully out of her control.

It felt so right and Joanna knew that whatever happened
she would have no regrets.

Joanna, naked and aroused, was the most beautiful vision
and the most sublime experience Richard had ever known.
They had both matured since the frenzied love-making of
their courtship and then the exhausting years of parenthood
that had followed when sex had slipped close to the bottom of
their priority list. It was like discovering each other all over
again. He gently ran his finger tips over the mallow-soft skin
of her breasts with their delicate web of veins; he yearned
for the lush and secret darkness of her and he delighted in
the perfect, smooth contours of her buttocks. There was no
doubt she had a magnificent body.

But she was much more than skin and flesh and bone.

Up until now she'd kept her inner beauty locked away,
showing only glimpses to those she felt needed it most.

Richard felt privileged she'd revealed her true self to him
in their exciting and startling love-making.

He hadn't planned it but, as he skimmed his fingers across
Joanna's belly and leaned over to kiss her cheek, he knew it
was meant to be.

'Are you okay?' he said softly as he clasped her hand and
eased his head back on the pillow. He watched the slow rise

and fall of her chest with each breath and marvelled at the perfection of the human form.

The gentle pressure from her hand was answer enough.

'I'm fine. It was good.' She opened her eyes and looked at him. 'Thank you, but you don't have to—'

'Shush.' He placed his fingers on her lips, not wanting to acknowledge that something so precious and uplifting could be transient. More than anything else in the world, he wanted to spend the rest of his days with Joanna.

'Let's think about tomorrow when it comes.'

She closed her eyes and brought his hand up to her lips, kissing his fingertips one by one.

'I don't think it's as easy as that.' She reached for the sheet, pulled it up to her waist and then rolled on her side to face him. She pressed his hand to her breast as if she wanted him to feel her heartbeat, to tune in to her life force.

'It's as easy or as difficult as you want to make it for yourself.' Richard knew from firsthand experience. It had been an agonising decision to leave Joanna but he'd believed it had been the best thing to do for both of them.

'But that's the problem.'

Her eyes were level with his but she was staring past him. She refocused with an intensity that was mesmerising.

'Problem?'

'We're still good together in bed—'

He smiled. 'I couldn't agree more.'

Her face was set and she wasn't in a joking mood so he refrained from saying anything else and waited for her to continue.

'Since you left I've really tried hard to keep my life as simple as I can make it.' She paused as if deciding whether she trusted him enough to go on. 'I've not let anyone get close to me since Sam died and…since you left. It's not worth it, all that heartache.' She took a deep sighing breath. 'I'm so sorry if I led you on, but I needed to know.'

She rolled onto her back again. Richard understood how the intimacy of their physical closeness could make what she was revealing difficult.

'To know?'

'Yes. To know if… How can I explain?'

'There's no need to explain. Me coming back, not knowing what to expect and having to decide whether to finally end our marriage. It must be—'

'Overwhelming. And I need to know that you are prepared to accept me for who I am now. I'm not the girl you married or the mixed-up woman who'd lost a child, a husband and a wonderful life with a future to look forward to—all in one fell swoop.'

She reached for his hand and gripped it with tense fingers.

'I know I said I wanted a divorce but I need time. All I know is that I still have feelings for you but I'm not sure if it could work, after all that's happened. If we try and start over we need to go very slowly.'

He appreciated the implications of what she was saying. And she'd opened herself to him. Given him something she held precious, and he realised he must be careful not to abuse her generosity.

'And you know it's unlikely I can have any more children.'

She said it as a simple statement of fact but he knew the words hung heavy with emotion. If anyone deserved a child— a truckload of children, in fact—it was Joanna.

He reached up and touched her cheek.

She pushed his hand away and folded her arms across her breasts.

'I'm sorry, Richard.'

'No.' He felt like shouting to make it clear to her there was no need to apologise. 'I'm the one who should be apologising.'

'Why?' She turned to face him again but held her body so they weren't touching. 'I have no regrets. About tonight, that is. It was wonderful.' She smiled and her whole face softened like a ripe peach on a warm day. 'Truly wonderful. But I don't want to start something I can't finish. I'm sorry.' She repeated the words softly.

They lay together without speaking for several long minutes.

'It doesn't matter to me whether I father children. It's you I care about.'

She sighed. 'You say that now but I know how much you loved Sam, and that you wanted more children—that I couldn't give you. You're capable of fathering as many as you want, but not with me. And your career choice… To do the job you do, you have to love kids.'

He knew that anything more he said to try and make her realise his life could be complete without children would fall on deaf ears.

'I agree, we both need time,' he said cautiously. 'And, whatever you decide, I'll go along with it. If you want to give it a go and it doesn't work out, then that's okay with me. If you need a few weeks, or months, just to think things through and you decide being married to me is not what you want then I'll go ahead and organise the divorce.' She seemed to be relaxing. He grinned, feeling the unexpected evidence of his physical desire return, and he was sure it hadn't gone unnoticed.

'And if you decided you wanted me to move in tomorrow I'd—'

She rewarded him with a twitch of her lips and a twinkle in her eye. Her hands caressed, her eyes teased and her body flushed a deliciously sexy shade of pink.

'Stop, I think you've made yourself perfectly clear,' she said. 'And I think you're right. I'm not ready to make a decision.' Her hand strayed to below his waist. 'But for now let's just seize the moment and let tomorrow take care of itself.

Joanna woke on Saturday morning alone and wondered if the events of the previous night had been a dream. The late summer sun streamed through her window as she basked in the heady contentment she'd always felt on the morning after satisfying love-making. But in the background was disappointment that Richard hadn't stayed. They'd both decided it was for the best, though. It would give them time to think things through.

He'd been right in suggesting they didn't rush into anything they'd regret and she certainly had no desire to launch into something as scary as attempting to take up where they'd left off. If they were to try to get to know each other again the process had to be a gradual one.

One careful step at a time.

Although the love-making had been fabulous, better than she remembered, she was certain that basing a relationship purely on good sex was asking for failure. She knew the statistics. One in three marriages in Australia ended in divorce.

It was something she didn't want to think about that morning, though. She rolled over, deciding to indulge in the luxury of staying in bed a little longer on her first day off in over a week. She was beginning to doze when the phone rang and jolted her back to full wakefulness. Grabbing her robe, she hurried into the living room and picked up the handpiece.

'Hello,' she said, half hoping it would be Richard, telling her he couldn't bear to be away from her, but it was a female voice.

'Hi, it's Lorraine. What are you doing this afternoon?'

A smile spread over Joanna's face. Lorraine Henderson

was the sort of person who tackled life head-on and definitely wasn't one to mince words. She'd emailed Joanna a couple of days ago to say she'd received permission from the hospital's medical director to go ahead with her plans to film the children for the concert. Apparently the request had generated the usual hefty volume of paperwork—documents to be prepared explaining the how, why, when and where; consent forms to be filled out by patients' families; permission to be obtained from the senior staff of each ward involved; disclaimers, and so on.... Joanna thought it would take weeks to sort out.

Maybe she had underestimated her friend's ability to move things along. She couldn't think of any other reason Lorraine would ring her at ten o'clock on a Saturday morning.

'Nothing, and I bet I can guess why you're asking. Something to do with the concert?'

Her friend chuckled. 'How did you know?'

'It's consuming all your spare time, isn't it? What's happening today?'

Lorraine paused as if she needed a moment to organise her thoughts.

'Steve's got a free afternoon to give us a hand with the camera work and I've managed to get all the paperwork sorted to start on Matilda Ward.' She paused only long enough to take a breath. 'And since it's your patch, and you seemed pretty keen about the idea, I thought you might like to be involved in our maiden shoot.'

Joanna laughed. The woman's enthusiasm was contagious.

'You've sussed out the talent, have you?'

'Sort of. Karen, your innovative play therapist, has already organised the littlies who are well enough to sing a couple of nursery songs. She said she'd get some costumes together for the final shoot but she's coming in today and it would be an ideal trial run. And when we get there we'll see if any of the older kids want to be involved.' She chuckled. 'If they don't want to perform Steve said we could lure them with technology.'

'Technology?'

'As well as his state-of-the-art, high-tech camera, he's bringing a couple of smaller camcorders he's happy to lend, under supervision of course. He also said if any of the older patients show interest or ability they could get involved in the editing later on. We've actually been given a tiny room in Admin. It has a desk and is lockable so it may come in handy for, at the very least, a storage area.'

'Wow, you've been working hard. And Steve's being amazingly generous. I'd love to come and help. What time?'

'Does around two o'clock sound all right? It's a time that would cause the least disruption to the ward.'

'Yep, sounds great. I'll see you then.'

Lorraine's invitation to go to the hospital gave Joanna a focus for her day and she was looking forward to the challenge of prising talent from the disparate group of small patients on Matilda Ward.

After breakfast she went to the nearest supermarket and stocked up with food and other essentials for the week ahead. On her way out she lingered at the newsagent and finally bought a fashion magazine. She then paused in front of a boutique displaying a new range of autumn clothing. The trend seemed to be feminine skirts, loosely flowing tops and lacy patterned knitwear in soft, warm colours. It had been a while since she'd bought any clothes, and these days she spent most of her time when she wasn't working in jeans, or shorts and T-shirts. A feminine outfit would make a change and seemed to suit the cheerful mood she was in that day.

She decided to unload her shopping in her car and go back and have a closer look.

Half an hour later she emerged from the boutique with a bagful of purchases and headed off to seek out a shoe store.

When she got home she unloaded her groceries and then spread the new clothes on her bed. After much vacillation, she still couldn't decide what to wear that afternoon. It somehow seemed important that she get it right. After all, she might be on camera and it made a change from her everyday uniform. She even considered wearing make-up.

After a late lunch and lengthy deliberation on what outfit to wear, she finally decided on a skirt with a subtle pattern in muted cream, ginger and peach and a simple sleeveless cream top. By the time she'd changed, it was time to leave for the hospital.

Richard heard the clapping and cheerful whooping before he entered the ward and paused in wonderment at the end-less resourcefulness of the nursing staff. He'd had an un-usual phone call that morning from the woman Joanna had mentioned was involved in producing the film segments for the concert.

'I need your signature on some papers before we can go ahead. Is that all right with you?' she'd asked. She was a woman not frightened of cutting to the chase and he imag-ined she would be a formidable rival if you found yourself on a team opposing her.

'Yes, that's fine. Shall we make a time on Monday—?'

'Um… If we could somehow get it done today… You see, Steve is available this afternoon and I was hoping…'

'Steve? Should I know who he is?' Lorraine was coming across as used to getting her own way but he admired her ability to get things done.

'He's my husband, our cameraman.' She paused but for only a moment. 'I could bring the documents to your house if that's more convenient.'

'No, I can meet you at the hospital…' He checked his electronic organiser on his phone and noticed he had the whole day free.

'Lunchtime. We could meet in the canteen, or up on the ward if you'd prefer.'

'I'd prefer the ward.'

'Right, Steve and I will see you at about one-thirty.'

He arrived at Matilda at twenty past and, as well as being noisy, the playroom looked like the venue for an elaborate children's party. Helium-filled balloons of all shapes and sizes bobbed and floated and a low table was loaded with rainbow-coloured party food. Hand-made streamers looped and tumbled around the windows. There was no indication that illness had had any effect to dampen the enthusiasm of about half a dozen pint-sized, noisy dynamos. Lorraine, Karen, a nurse Richard hadn't met and a tall, thin, bearded man he assumed was Lorraine's husband were bustling around trying, unsuccessfully, to instil some kind of order into the joyful chaos. Parents were dotted around the room, chatting and smiling.

It was truly a wonderful sight.

After letting one of the ward sisters know he was there, he made his way to the glass-walled playroom and lingered in the doorway, and it wasn't long before he was spotted.

'Dotta Howl!' Leisha, aged three and a half and on crutches, launched herself at him. She discarded her walking aids and hugged his knee with the strength of a child twice her age. She'd adapted amazingly well to her mid-thigh amputation and was due for discharge the following week.

He reached down to hug the girl and she managed to plant a sloppy kiss on his cheek before Karen whisked her away.

Then Lorraine saw him and greeted him with a broad grin.

'Thank you so much for coming. We all really appreciate it.' He looked around the room and acknowledged a few of the parents he recognised.

'No problem. Maybe we could go somewhere quieter to do the paperwork,' he said as Lorraine retrieved a folder from the top of a tall cupboard, safely out of reach of her small charges.

'Good idea,' she said.

Fifteen minutes later all the formalities were complete and Richard got up to leave the tutorial room. Suddenly, the thought of going home to a coldly impersonal, empty house held no attraction for him and he wanted to be involved in the rowdy pandemonium that was happening down the corridor.

'When do you actually start filming?' he said tentatively.

'If Steve can manage to find a space to set up his gear, hopefully in about half, maybe three quarters of an hour.' She smiled. 'You're welcome to stay and watch if you want. If you're hungry and don't mind fairy bread, peanut-butter pinwheels and fruit jelly for lunch...'

'I think I'll pass. I might go over to the doctors' dining room for something to eat and come back.'

'Wonderful. The more the merrier, but don't expect to stand on the sidelines. I'm sure we'll be able to find something for you to do.'

And with a flurry she was off, humming what he guessed was a slightly out-of-tune rendition of 'Raindrops Keep Falling on My Head'.

When he came back half an hour later, a little more order prevailed in the playroom. It was relatively quiet, though the numbers seemed to have swelled. In the few moments before Karen grabbed him and led him over to a group of parents who seemed to be involved in some sort of artwork, he gazed around the room. His eyes stopped and fixed on the gorgeous, dark-eyed woman with a toddler on her knee.

She was truly beautiful.

Centimetre-long, jet-black hair contrasted with the softly

tanned skin of her face, reminding him of an olden-time porcelain doll. Her swirling full skirt fell below her knees and he could see her underwear—a lace-edged camisole—through her almost transparent blouse. The outfit left just enough to the imagination to make it tantalisingly seductive.

She looked like an angel cradling a cherub and the vision took his breath away.

All he wanted to do at that moment was scoop Joanna into his arms, hold her body close to his and pray she could find it in her heart to at least try to love him.

'Quiet, everyone.' Steve's clear, authoritative voice managed to still even the most boisterous child. 'Ready to go.' Lorraine then scissored her arms in the air, mimicking a clapper board and Joanna began to sing.

The toddler on her knee, the other patients, their parents and the staff were all mesmerised as Jo's clear, pure voice filled every corner of the room. Richard heard few of the words of the bouncy little song, though. The lyrics didn't seem to matter. What really mattered was that Joanna's total attention was focused on the child. The expression on her face, the look in her eyes were straight out of the past.

The memories flooded back to happier times and it was as if Sam was again snuggled up to her, as if she was pouring the deep love she had for their son into her song.

It was as if Sam was still alive.

The room began to close in on him, faces blurring, sounds becoming fuzzy and indistinct. Richard cleared his throat, stood on shaky legs and did his utmost to quietly leave the room before Joanna noticed him. Once he was out of sight he slumped against the wall and wiped away a tear—the first tear he'd shed since his son had died.

When Joanna finished the song, she realised the occupants of the room, even the babies, were totally silent and their attention was focused on her. She felt the flush of embarrassment rush from her neck to her cheeks. She'd been so absorbed in the song, and the living, breathing bundle of life sitting on her lap, she'd blocked out everything else.

'That was *so* moving.' Karen came over and gave Joanna a hug and, to her relief, a buzz of conversation began again. She wasn't used to being the centre of attention and felt acutely uncomfortable. She released a nervous laugh.

'How can you say "The Easter Bunny Song" is moving?'

Karen looked at her searchingly.

'Well, I reckon Dr Howell was touched.'

What on earth was Karen talking about? Richard had nothing to do with the song. An uneasy thought entered Joanna's mind that Karen knew…knew they were married or at least had some kind of personal relationship happening. Karen was still staring at her with a half-smile on her face.

'Dr Howell? What do you mean?'

Karen hoisted Leisha, who was grizzling quietly and was obviously tired, onto her hip. The little girl yawned.

'He was here a minute ago and left in a hurry. He looked as if he was…um…'

Several alarming thoughts skittered through Joanna's mind. What was Richard doing in the ward on the weekend in the first place? She knew he wasn't on call. Had he hinted at a relationship between them without realising the ramifications, particularly if they decided to go ahead with the divorce?

Had he let her down?

Now the conversation with Karen had got this far, though, she needed to know what was going through the play therapist's mind. She didn't want to be the topic of unsubstantiated gossip; she valued her privacy when it came to her life outside the workplace.

'How did he look?' Joanna surprised herself with the hard edge to her voice.

'If you want my honest opinion, I'd say he was close to tears.' There was nothing in Karen's tone of voice or the expression on her face to suggest she was joking. She looked deadly serious.

'And he left a few moments ago?'

'That's right.'

Leisha began grizzling again and Karen looked around the room to see if the girl's mother had returned from taking Leisha's twin brother to the toilet. She spotted her on the other side of the room, cuddling another unhappy pre-schooler.

'I'm going to have to leave you to it. I think it's time to get these over-excited kids back to their beds for a rest.'

Joanna welcomed the distraction of the now restless children and took the opportunity to slip away—she hoped, unnoticed. Karen's words kept repeating in her mind.

I'd say he was close to tears.

But Richard never cried.

She'd often wondered if their marriage would have had a second chance if they'd been able to cry together, to grieve together, to share the emotional devastation that had wreaked havoc in their lives nearly four long years ago.

Joanna thought she'd moved on, but had Richard?

Close to tears.

She knew him well enough to know what would bring up the pain of the past. There was no other reason she could think of for why he would become noticeably emotional—a man who could always keep his feelings in check. To break down in public would be the worst humiliation imaginable.

Joanna needed to see Richard, even if it meant paging him and saying it was an emergency.

She hurried out of the ward, ran to catch the lift before the door closed and tried to formulate in her mind what she would do, what she would say to him if…when she tracked him down.

She didn't need to ruminate for very long, though.

When the lift reached the ground floor and the doors opened, she almost collided with him as he strode through the entrance to the stairwell. His head was down and he seemed so determined to get out of the building he didn't notice her.

'Richard.' It was barely a whisper. She quickly swallowed the stubborn lump that had formed in her throat.

'Richard!' she shouted as she broke into a run.

He stopped and turned as the automatic doors began to close and was unable to contain the look of surprise on his face. Joanna could see no sign of tears but could tell he was upset. A shard of anger appeared in his eyes but was replaced by his normal control in the time it took him to blink.

Why was he angry?

She understood why he would be upset, but the anger confused her, and while she hesitated he backtracked and walked towards her.

'Joanna, what a coincidence. It's great to see you.'

He obviously had no idea she knew he'd been on Matilda Ward while she'd been singing.

She grasped his hand and pulled him close enough for him to hear her whisper.

'I need to talk to you, Richard.'

He lifted his eyebrows as if her request had taken him by surprise.

'Here? Now?'

'No, Richard.'

Somewhere private where tears won't cause loss of face.

'It's a…er…sensitive matter that I think needs privacy to discuss.'

He hesitated for a moment or two. 'Would you like to go back to my place, then?' he said, his smile erasing any remnants of distress. She refused to read anything between the lines of the invitation, though. It seemed a reasonable request.

'Yes, Richard. That would suit me fine.' She readjusted her bag on her shoulder and began to walk towards the doors. She'd heard he'd moved into one of the doctors' houses a couple of streets away. That suited her. It was on her way home and it meant she didn't have to depend on Richard for a lift.

'Did you walk?' she asked as they set off on one of the meandering pathways that ended up at the back of the hospital. Richard adjusted his usual long stride to her slower pace. He glanced in her direction.

'Yes, I moved into Peppermint Mews the weekend after I started at Lady Lawler. It's only five minutes away.' He paused. 'You'll be my first guest.'

Joanna wanted to spout a witty reply but she couldn't think of anything appropriate to say and they walked the rest of the way in edgy silence. Unfortunately it provided an opportunity for Joanna to think and she began wondering if she'd made a mistake. What would she say? Just come right out with it—that Karen told her she thought he had been on the verge of tears? Or skirt around the edge of the issue? Hope that he'd pick up on her concerns without having to spell it out?

But it was too late now to bail out.

They reached the block of terraces where Richard lived and he stopped at the gate of the house second from the end. It was identical to all of the others apart from the colour of the front door—his was a glossy navy blue—and the contents of the front garden. Richard's was crazy paved and decorated with a couple of terracotta pots containing a pair of struggling geraniums.

'This is it,' Richard said as he opened the gate for her.

'It doesn't suit you.' Her comment, though bold, was the truth.

'I know. You're absolutely right.' He ran his fingers through his hair. 'It's only temporary until I find something better.' He stepped into the tiny portico and unlocked the door. To Joanna's surprise he looked embarrassed. 'And I take no credit for the decorating.' In a roundabout way he was apologising for his humble, short-term lodgings, which surprised her. He'd never paid much attention to keeping up appearances.

'Come in and sit down,' he added, indicating a doorway, one of several opening off a central passage that led to what looked like a kitchen-dining area. She presumed the bedrooms were upstairs. 'Can I get you something to drink?'

'Just water for me, thanks.'

Joanna wasn't thirsty but wanted a minute or two to compose herself. Richard left the room and headed towards the back of the house. She took a couple of deep breaths and glanced around the room and her gaze froze when she saw the photos on the mantle above the fireplace—for all the world to see.

Oh, my God!

Her heart began to race.

She recognised both snapshots. They were displayed in a decorative, hinged silver frame and were the only homely touch in what Joanna viewed as a comfortable though boring room.

She picked up the frame and examined the photos more closely. The first was a head-and-shoulders portrait of her and Richard on their wedding day. It wasn't a professional shot but the photographer had captured the essence of their mood, which was a heady mix of joy, laughter, and unquestionable love for each other. Richard was gazing at her with a big goofy grin on his face and stars in his eyes. She, at twenty, looked so young and innocent but she was beaming with happiness and waving at the camera.

The second photo was at the beach. Joanna must have taken the picture but, although she remembered the day vividly, she didn't remember recording it on film. It showed Richard and Sam and it was also brimming with the joy of living. Richard was chest deep in the water and held his precious son in his arms. You could easily see that Sam was smiling as he reached out to touch the graceful dolphin gliding by. It was the last time they had taken their son to the beach—the last time before the cruel disease had taken his life. And it was as if the beautiful, intuitive creature knew Sam didn't have much time left and had come to say goodbye.

Joanna wiped a tear from her cheek and put the photos back at the same moment Richard walked into the room. She stood in front of the fireplace, not knowing what to do or say. Her visit that afternoon was supposed to be about trying to free Richard's cloistered emotions, but she was the one who couldn't hold back the tears. She sniffed and moved over to the couch where Richard had placed a tray.

'What's the matter?' His look was razor sharp and soft as duck down all at once. It cut through her defences and stripped her of the calm control she'd learned, from her husband, to wear like a suit of armour. 'Have you been crying?'

She shrugged. The question was unnecessary. He could easily see the tears smeared on her face.

'The...the photos...' she faltered.

'They are the only family shots I have.' He stood with his hands in the pockets of his jeans and looked past Joanna. His eyes lost focus and he swallowed.

'When I left, I thought I'd be coming back...to you. I needed a break and I thought time would heal at least some of the hurt.'

He sat down next to her, fixing his searching eyes on her

face. He reached for her hand and she didn't resist his firm and consoling grasp. *He* had taken the role of comforter away from her and claimed it for himself. Jo knew that role usually came with unspoken permission to store his feelings in an inaccessible box; to do the job he'd been trained to do, regardless of whether it was at the expense of dealing with his own anguish. He could then concentrate on the task of healing and reassuring others...*covering old wounds with a veil of optimism.*

No, not this time.

Joanna was unable to contemplate a life with Richard if he couldn't be open with her. Trust and communication were two essential characteristics in any relationship. One of the reasons why she and Richard had parted had been that they had stopped communicating. Joanna realised, too late, that she'd been as much to blame as him.

But she hoped she'd learned from her mistakes. The opportunity to start over opened up the way to getting it right this time.

Or getting it very wrong.

Joanna couldn't afford to take that risk.

Sometimes love wasn't enough and she would rather spend the rest of her life alone than with a man who felt he had to be strong for her all the time.

She finally broke the silence.

'Those photos represent two of the most important turning points in our relationship.' Richard waited for her reply cloaked with an unreadable expression. 'The beginning of our marriage, our long-term commitment to each other and...' Jo knew what she wanted to say but the words stuck in her throat.

'And?'

'And the end of our marriage.' There, she'd said it. Their life together had fallen apart when they had lost their child.

Sam had turned out to be the sustenance of their love and it was only when he'd gone that the full impact had struck. Neither of them had had the strength to do battle with their own demons, let alone share their grief. Joanna had cocooned herself in despair and Richard... She knew he'd tried his best but it hadn't been enough. In being the strong one, he'd buried part of himself. He'd buried his own guilt and pain and devastation. Joanna could see that now and was grateful for how hard he'd tried to help, but it hadn't made sense to her at the time.

She'd wanted him to cry therapeutic tears with her, to share the load so they could carry it forward, together. Not ignore their problems and maintain an outwardly happy face in the name of toughing it out.

Richard's thumb traced a pattern on the palm of her hand with warm, gentle pressure.

'I tried so hard—'

'I know. But maybe you tried too hard. You never broke down. You were always the tower of strength. But what I needed was to see that you were as vulnerable as me. In the end you seemed to almost stop being human.'

'It was the only way I knew to cope.' The dark pupils of his deep blue eyes dilated and Joanna thought she detected a slight tremor in his hand. It was the reassurance she needed. He was on the brink of sharing his feelings.

'But you still do it, Richard. I don't think you've...' But she couldn't say it. She didn't know how to tell her husband she thought he hadn't yet worked through the grieving process necessary to move on. She suspected it was the reason he'd stayed away so long; it had probably been an escape for him, to a life full of strangers and distractions and a full-on workload.

Richard opened his mouth to speak but closed it again.

'Do you want me to forget we had a son?' he finally said, his voice a husky whisper.

'No, of course I don't. There's not a day goes past that I don't think about Sam. He was an important part of our lives. Still is. But I realise it serves no purpose to let the memories overwhelm me. It's taken me a long time to realise that.' She took a deep breath in an effort to give herself the courage to continue. 'And my work in Oncology has helped.'

Richard reached across for the bottle of spring water he'd brought in on the tray. He opened it and half filled both glasses. He took one for himself and offered the other to Joanna but she refused. The dryness she felt in her throat wouldn't be relieved by water.

'Yes, I know.' Richard swallowed a mouthful of his drink. 'Anyone can see how much you care for the kids on Matilda.'

'It makes it easier when I know how difficult it would be to fall pregnant.'

Richard's gaze lowered and he rubbed the back of his neck as if to massage away a ball of tension. Then he looked up.

'So what do you want me to do, Joanna? I can't change who I am. I can't change the past.'

She looked at him for a long moment and realised the only answer she could give was the truth.

'I still love you, Richard. I want us to try again. But it won't work if we can't share the bad times as well as the good. I know the memory of Sam will always be there and I want…' She took a sip of water while Richard waited for her to continue. 'I want you to let yourself cry for Sam.'

He stood up and walked over to the window that faced the street. He leaned on the sill with his arms spread wide. At least he was thinking about what she'd said. He hadn't dismissed her words as being sentimental nonsense. The barrier hadn't gone up yet.

Finally he turned.

'I can't turn on tears for you, Jo.'

'I don't expect you to. I just want to know you are able to... How can I say it...? You're able to give yourself permission.'

He walked back to where she was sitting, leaned forward and kissed her gently on the forehead.

'I'm not sure I can do what you want, but I'm prepared to try.'

CHAPTER EIGHT

NIGHT shifts weren't usually a problem for Joanna but now she was nearing the end of her month-long stint the days were dragging. She was counting the shifts until she finished, looking forward to starting work in daylight hours and going to bed after sunset. She knew nursing involved around-the-clock care but the busy, hands-on day shifts suited her better than the usually quiet and uneventful nights.

And, of course, she would see more of Richard when her roster changed.

His attitude seemed more relaxed as they took the first tentative steps to get to know each other again. He'd said little about their heart-to-heart talk but she was perceptive enough to notice his attitude towards her had changed. The spark was still there but they'd both agreed to take things slowly.

The tongues of the hospital grapevine had already started to wag, though, which wasn't surprising because it was difficult to disguise the fact that their relationship went further than a straightforward professional association between nurse and consultant. She hadn't yet decided whether the gossip was a good or bad thing, but at least no one knew about their past. Joanna had enough to deal with without having to cope with the possibility of endless questions, probably associated with well-meant but unwelcome sympathy.

The combination of Joanna working night shifts and

Richard's busy schedule meant they'd had little opportunity for one-to-one contact. He'd walked her home from choir rehearsals a couple of times but she'd been shy of asking him in. The closest they'd come to a date had been his invitation for her to come swimming with him after work. They'd also shared a meal with the 'film crew' the previous Saturday after helping Lorraine and Steve with the final shoot of the Matilda Ward segment for the concert. But that didn't count because they'd been part of a large, noisy and excited group and had barely spoken to each other.

The concert.

It was only two weeks away and preparations were going well. The performance was scheduled for Easter Saturday and Richard had promised to take Joanna out on a *proper date* on the following evening.

To celebrate, he'd said mysteriously.

To celebrate what?

Of course, the predicted success of the concert was cause for celebration but the look in his eye when he'd invited her suggested he had more than the hospital fundraiser on his mind.

He'd told her he'd already booked a table for two at a fancy, waterside restaurant but he wouldn't tell her where. She was looking forward to it and had bought a new dress in honour of the occasion.

She smiled as she walked back to the nurses' station after doing her 6:00 a.m. rounds. It was her last night shift for at least another three months and she was dog tired. The previous day she'd found it difficult to sleep and as a result had felt overtired and cranky before she'd even started her shift. This stint had taken its toll more than usual and in the last hour she'd resorted to watching the clock. She yawned and followed it up with a deep, sighing breath.

'What's up, Jo?' Barbara asked. The ward was quiet and

they had time to share a cup of tea. She must have noticed the number of times Joanna had yawned that night. 'You look like the subject of a sleep deprivation experiment.'

Joanna managed a smile.

'Funny you should say it. That's just how I feel.'

'So what's going on with Matilda Ward's very own Miss Cheerfulness? What's caused you to lose some of your shine?'

Joanna tried to suppress another yawn but without success. She sipped her tea, hoping it would revive her. Although she appreciated the older woman's concern, she liked to keep her private life to herself.

'I'm fine. Just a bit tired. I've been lucky up until now, being able to sleep during the day. Quiet street, neighbours who work—'

Barbara was looking at her with a quizzical, motherly expression, but seemed happy with the answer. The supervisor went back to her work, checking that the medication doses and times had been filled in correctly. She checked and double-checked. The hospital was currently cracking down on record-keeping, particularly regarding medications, after a near fatal mistake in the emergency department.

'Anything else I can do?' Joanna said, suppressing another yawn.

The concerned look Barbara gave her said more than words.

'If you weren't at the end of your stint on nights, I'd recommend you take a couple of days' leave. Are you sure you're not coming down with something?'

'Really, Barbara…' She attempted to laugh off the fact that she felt dead on her feet. 'Maybe I'm just starting to feel my age.'

'All right, but how about you go home early? It's only an hour and I can sign you off as being unwell. You're not much use to us in your state and the ward's really quiet. Tracey and I can hold the fort.'

'No, I'll be fine.' She could count the number of sick days she'd had over her entire nursing career on the fingers of one hand. She wasn't about to take time off because she'd had trouble sleeping. And it wasn't as if she didn't know the reason. 'And I assure you I won't let a couple of extra yawns interfere with my work,' she added.

Barbara was studying her intently.

'You look pale.'

'I'm okay, really I am.'

'Not feeling a bit queasy, are you?'

'No. Is there a bug going around that I don't know about?'

Barbara smiled, got up to replace the charts in the trolley and patted her on the shoulder.

'There's always a bug going around in this place. It's a hospital isn't it?'

'You're not wrong, Barb.' Another yawn threatened. Joanna picked up a magazine and began flipping through it. Barbara went over to the cooler and poured herself half a cup of water to swallow the blood-pressure tablet she always took at six o'clock. She stood silently for a minute or so, as if deep in thought.

'You're not pregnant, are you?' she finally asked.

Fat chance, in fact no chance at all.

It must have been her weariness, the culmination of a series of unusual events over the last week, and she knew she should be laughing at Barb's well-intentioned inquiry.

Joanna looked over at Barbara.

'No, I'm not pregnant.' She had to work hard at stopping her voice from shaking.

'How can you be sure?'

'Anatomically impossible, I'm afraid,' Joanna, the clinical, rational nurse managed to say in a rock-steady voice. 'My tubes are blocked. I had a ruptured appendix when I was six-teen…'

'Oh, Jo, I honestly didn't know.'

'Of course you didn't. I don't go broadcasting…' Then Joanna burst into tears and couldn't stop sobbing. Barbara wrapped her arms around her.

'You poor love. I insist you go home and I'll arrange a taxi. You can't stay here like this.'

Joanna didn't have the energy to protest.

A good, solid, uninterrupted nine hours' sleep made all the difference to how Joanna felt. It was as if she'd been born again and the events of the morning hadn't happened, or at least had diminished to a hazy, distant blur.

Her only problem was that she had slept so well during the day she was unlikely to sleep that night. She knew she should have set her alarm to help her inbuilt rhythm restore itself but with all that had happened, she'd forgotten—and it wasn't the end of the world.

She gathered clean underwear, the new peach-coloured towelling robe she'd treated herself to the previous week and headed to the bathroom. The cake of hand-made apple and al-mond soap she hadn't been able to resist at the market smelled delicious and almost edible. She felt she had not a care in the world.

It was a warm evening so, after her shower, she dressed in casual knee-length shorts and a T-shirt and actually ran a comb through her centimetre-long hair. It made little dif-ference, though. Her hair refused to be persuaded to do any-thing but stick up at a right angle to her scalp.

After fortifying herself with a good strong cup of tea, she decided to go for a walk. She felt she needed an extra-strong dose of fresh air after a month of working nights and sleep-ing for three quarters of the day. She hoped an hour or so of exercise would help her sleep at least a few hours that night, although it usually took a couple of days for her normal diurnal rhythm to get back to normal. She also decided to pick up some take-away on the way back. Putting a twenty-dollar note in her pocket, she grabbed her broad-brimmed hat and strode out of her little house. She followed the quaint, brick-paved laneway that fronted the property to the main road and then headed for the park a couple of blocks away.

Joanna started off walking at a fairly brisk pace but began to tire by the time she reached the park so she slowed down. The sun was sinking lower and a gentle breeze cooled the early evening air. She enjoyed strolling along the path that circled a haphazard string of pools and small lakes. She smiled at a middle-aged man who was being dragged along by a boisterous young German shepherd, and stopped to chat briefly to a couple proudly pushing tiny twins in a contraption that looked like it was ready to take off for outer space.

'They're beautiful,' Joanna said as she leaned forward to take a closer look at the sleeping babies, both dressed in white. 'Are they boys, girls or one of each?'

'Girls, only a month old,' was all the beaming father managed to say before his wife interrupted.

'And they're not identical,' the young mum said.

'They look very similar.' In fact, it was difficult for Jo to tell them apart. Her heart swelled for the couple. 'What are their names?'

'Emily and Victoria, after their grandmothers.'

A tiny splinter of jealousy niggled in Joanna's mind but she dismissed the thought quickly. She'd long ago accepted that motherhood wasn't going to be part of her life again.

'I'll let you get on with your stroll.'

The woman linked her arm in her husband's. They set off in the opposite direction and, from that instant, Joanna's mood subtly changed. She couldn't help thinking of Richard and his declaration of love. Had he fully thought things through? If they *did* manage to resurrect their marriage, would there always be something missing? Richard was physically able to father a child but had told her it didn't matter to him if their future didn't include children. But Joanna couldn't help wondering if she'd feel guilty for depriving him of something she knew was important to him.

And she couldn't cope with IVF. Not now. The journey would be too painful for her and she knew the failure rate was relatively high.

And what if she did become pregnant? She wasn't sure she'd be able to go through a pregnancy that might end in a miscarriage or stillbirth or, even worse, result in a living, breathing perfect child that was taken from them...

She couldn't do it.

By the time she'd walked two circuits of the park she was tiring again. Her heart thudded in her chest, queasiness niggled in her stomach and she'd lost her appetite. She was now feeling tense halfway through a walk that was supposed to relax and energise her. Suddenly she felt light-headed and looked around for a seat. There was a park bench at the water's edge, a few metres away. When she reached it her legs felt like jelly as she sank onto the seat.

What was wrong? Was she having some kind of anxiety attack?

She'd never had one before.

She took a few slow, deep breaths but it didn't make much difference.

The only time in her life she'd felt anything like this had been when she'd been pregnant with Sam.

Pregnant with Sam...

Pregnant.

Could she be?

No, of course she couldn't. She'd had tests and she was

infertile. She and Richard had never used contraception because there'd been no point.

But...

She'd managed to fall pregnant at age nineteen, against all
the odds.

Her heart was now pounding and her head ached but she
needed to start thinking rationally or her outlandish suppo-
sitions would consume her.

When was her last period? She never kept a record because there'd been no need but she knew her cycle was regular. And it had been a while, certainly before she'd started
working nights. She racked her brain and then recalled her
last period had been around the time Richard had started at
Lady Lawler.

She did the calculations.

Oh, my God.

She and Richard had made love about two weeks later and
she hadn't had a period since. Which had been well over a
month ago.

'So if I'm pregnant, I'd be six or seven weeks,' she whispered, not quite believing what her mind and body were telling her.

But how unlikely was that?

The odds were stacked so heavily against her... A nervous
laugh surfaced from somewhere deep in her throat.

More slow breaths.

She fingered the twenty-dollar note in her pocket. There
was a late-opening pharmacy on her way home. If she was
to get any sleep that night she had to know.

The pharmacist, the only person in attendance in the small
shop, was a dark-skinned man, who looked several years
younger than her. There were a number of people waiting to
be served and an elderly couple, who were trying out walk-

ing sticks, took up most of the central aisle space. Joanna heard the young man explain to the woman at the head of the queue that his assistant had had a family emergency and had to leave. He was waiting for her replacement. He looked harassed and Joanna began to have second thoughts.

But she had to know.

As soon as was practically possible.

Once she'd confirmed that the test was negative she'd be able to relax and the troublesome symptoms of her uncertainty would go away.

She decided to wait and, after ten, long, agonising minutes, her turn came.

'Yes, what can I do for you?' To his credit the pharmacist attempted a smile.

'I want a home pregnancy test kit.'

'Dip or stream?'

'Pardon?' What on earth did he mean? Despite her nursing background, she had no idea what he was talking about.

He lowered his voice. 'Do you want to dip into a specimen cup or just pee on the stick?'

Joanna was acutely aware that the other occupants of the shop could hear every word. She felt the heat rise to her neck and was glad she hadn't removed her hat.

'Whichever is most accurate...' She had a quick thought. She had no idea how much the tests cost. 'And costs less than twenty dollars.'

A look of sympathy crossed the man's face but it didn't change the fact he still looked about eighteen to Joanna.

The man glanced behind her as if reminding her there were other people waiting, but she'd got this far and she wasn't going to chicken out now.

'It depends on how far along you are.' The guy was assuming she *was* pregnant and it unsettled her even more.

'Um…' The conversation was turning into an ordeal. 'About six weeks, I think.'

'They're all between ninety-five and ninety-nine per cent accurate at that stage.' To her relief the inquisition stopped and he moved to scan a shelf to one side of the counter. He selected a couple of boxes.

'This is a popular one. Easy to use and to read. You can buy it in a single pack for seven ninety-five or in the double for fifteen dollars.

She handed him the money. 'I'll take the double.'

At that moment, a middle-aged woman in a pale blue uniform burst into the shop with a flurry.

'I can take over now, Ramesh. I'm sure you have some scripts to do.'

The pharmacist, looking relieved, nodded as the assistant took the twenty-dollar note from one hand and the test kit from the other. He made his way onto the platform overlooking the shop, where the prescriptions were made up. The woman glanced at the box and then at Joanna.

'Just this?'

'Yes, thanks.'

The woman completed the transaction, placed the purchase in a small paper bag and handed it to Joanna with her change.

Joanna nearly bowled over a wandering toddler as she left and had never been more relieved in her life to get out of a shop.

Twenty minutes later she was standing in her kitchen, ripping off the packaging of the pregnancy test kit. She unfolded the instructions and spread the single sheet of paper on the bench. Words blurred in and out of focus.

'Concentrate!' she muttered. 'You don't want to stuff this up.'

She read the instructions.

Absorbent tip pointing downward...
...urine stream for five seconds...
Wait three minutes before reading results...
TWO PINK LINES...

Her gaze shifted from the diagram that showed the two lines to the one next to it.

NOT PREGNANT, ONE PINK LINE.

That was the result she was expecting and the instructions seemed simple enough. She took the test stick into the bathroom and when she finally stopped shaking managed to pee on the stick.

The next three minutes were the longest three minutes of her life.

She sat on the toilet lid with the tester in her right hand and her eyes fixed on the second hand of her watch on the other wrist. She decided not to look at the result until the time was up because she felt sure she would imagine lines and confuse herself.

'Ten, nine, eight...' She began a countdown back to zero and when she reached five her hand began to shake. 'Zero.'

Her eyes moved to the results window as she tried to steady her hand.

Right.

She focused.

Two pink lines. Yes, definitely two, so if the test was accurate she was pregnant with Richard's child.

Tears of happiness filled her eyes and vibrant warmth suffused her whole body.

She was pregnant with Richard's child.

Oh, dear God, what was she going to do?

A moment later all her fears descended on her like a landslide and she began to weep.

* * *

Richard was looking forward to the Tuesday morning ward round because Joanna was back on day shift. He'd missed her smiling face, her common-sense suggestions and her ability to make even the most despondent child laugh. He'd tried to contact her a couple of times on the weekend, hoping to meet up, maybe go on a picnic, but she hadn't answered her phone. Although he'd been disappointed, he didn't want to be pushy. At the last concert rehearsal they'd attended together just over a week ago, she'd seemed exhausted and she'd probably wanted a peaceful weekend to get her energy back.

When he entered Matilda Ward at just after eight o'clock, there was no sign of Joanna. Lynne had the trolley with all the patient notes ready, but was on the phone. She waved and mouthed the words, 'Won't be long.'

Richard nodded and used the time by having a quick look at Danny Sims's latest scan. He smiled. The bulk of his tumour had reduced by roughly twenty per cent, which was more than anyone had hoped for in such a short time. If he continued to respond so well to his chemotherapy, there was a good chance his prognosis would improve. A full remission was too much to hope for at this stage but it at least put a positive outcome for his treatment in the realms of possibility.

Lynne hung up the phone and summoned the student nurse, Tracey, to the nurses' station.

'Good morning, Richard,' the charge nurse said with a cheerful smile. 'Do you mind if Tracey comes with us on the round this morning?'

'No, of course not.' Richard tried to hide his disappointment. 'Where's Joanna? I thought she was back today.'

Lynne's eyebrows elevated. Maybe he hadn't disguised his disappointment as well as he'd hoped.

'Yes, she is. But she said she felt a bit off colour on the weekend so she's been designated as our runner. I decided, just as a precaution, to reduce her patient contact today. Just in case she has a virus and is contagious.'

Richard wanted to cross-examine Lynne as to what exactly was the matter with Jo but decided to find out for himself later. He'd attempt to catch up with her at some stage during the day and if that didn't happen, he'd call by her house after work. Maybe take some food. Yes, that was what he would do.

Lynne looked at him expectantly. He tried to look interested but not overly concerned.

'Your runner?' The question was in neutral territory. Richard hadn't heard that term used to describe the duties of a nurse before and was genuinely interested.

'I guess we use the term in the same way "girl Friday" is used in an office. She runs messages, does odd jobs, that sort of thing. She's doing an inventory of our storeroom at the moment.'

'Oh.' He paused and Lynne looked at him questioningly. 'We'd better get on with the round, then.'

The ward round went smoothly but took a little longer than usual because Lynne spent extra time explaining certain things to Tracey. Richard only glimpsed Joanna in passing a couple of times and on both occasions she had her head down and appeared not to notice him. He couldn't help thinking something was wrong and he wondered if he was to blame.

After the round he had a couple of referrals from other wards to follow up, which he set off to do mid-morning, and when he finished close to lunchtime he headed for the canteen. He bought his lunch and stayed half an hour but there was no sign of Joanna. Of course, at five o'clock when his afternoon clinic wound up, her shift would have finished and he lamented the fact he'd not even said hello to Jo over the full duration of her working day.

It was after six when he completed his paperwork and was

ready to go home. He realised how hungry he was when his stomach began to rumble so he walked home briskly to collect his car and drove to one of his favourite eateries, The Station Café, and emerged with a double serving of herbed lamb cutlets and three different kinds of salad. He hoped Joanna hadn't eaten already because he was looking forward to sharing a meal and part of the evening with her.

He parked in the street because he knew there was only space for one car in the short driveway off the lane. When he let himself in the gate he could see that Joanna was home because the television and lights were on. As he approached the back patio door he could see no sign of Joanna, though.

He knocked.

No answer.

He hammered on the door and called out but there was still no sign of life.

Maybe she'd gone out and left the television on.

As he turned to leave he heard movement, the noise of the TV silenced and Joanna appeared, damp and wrapped in a towelling robe. She eased the slider open just enough for her to talk to him but it looked like she had no intention of inviting him in.

He held up the bags of food as a peace offering.

'From The Station Café. I hope you're hungry.'

She still didn't open the door.

'I'm sorry, Richard, but I've already eaten and what I really need is an early night. I haven't been sleeping well over the last couple of nights.' She hesitated. 'I just need to be by myself.'

She definitely did look tired…and pale…and unwell.

'What's the matter, Jo? Are you sick?'

Her mouth set in a thin line and she shook her head.

'Really, I'm just tired and I…' She yawned and rubbed her reddened eyes. Had she been crying? Why had she suddenly

closed herself off from him when he'd thought their relationship was beginning to blossom? She'd at least been friendly
towards him during the few times they'd been together over
the past couple of weeks. He'd been careful not to encroach
too much on her personal space and he'd intentionally let her
set the pace.

Which for him, at times, had been painfully slow.

Had she changed her mind?

'Maybe we can have dinner together another evening.' Her
expression was unconvincing. 'If you let me know. Give me
some notice.' She attempted a smile but didn't quite pull it
off.

'I'm sorry.' She paled, her hand moved to her stomach and
then she closed the door and walked away from him.

There was definitely something wrong but he knew how
stubborn she could be. If she didn't want to talk about it, there
was nothing he could do to help.

Joanna had felt queasy all day but she suspected it had nothing
to do with her pregnancy and more to do with stress. She'd
repeated the test that morning, this time staring defiantly at
the little window that showed the result and the second line
had started to appear after about thirty seconds. She'd also
noticed her breasts had begun to tingle and she seemed to be
peeing more often. And as for her mental state… She felt per-
manently on the verge of tears, totally confused as to whether
she was pleased or distraught about her condition and coming to the conclusion it was a mix of both.

She needed to tell Richard, but she wasn't ready now.
During her shift she'd intentionally avoided any contact with
him and when he'd arrived on her doorstep she'd felt like
pleading with him to simply go away and leave her alone.
Although she'd not followed her impulse to turn him away,

she suspected Richard knew she wasn't her normal, happy, cope-with-anything-and-everything self.

But she definitely wasn't ready.

She needed time to think things through.

'When all else fails, have a cup of tea,' she muttered as she boiled the kettle and made herself a strong, sweet brew. Then she turned the television onto a chat show she usually found both funny and entertaining. The regular music segment was on and this week it was a jazz band. The musicians were playing a foot-tapping contemporary number as backing for a beautiful, young female singer.

It reminded her how quickly the concert was approaching. The final rehearsal was less than a week away. Not long, but it would give her an incentive to try and sort out the turmoil in her mind.

She would tell Richard about her pregnancy on Easter Sunday. On their dinner date.

Yes, that's what she would do—tell him after the concert.

The concert was a sell-out and, strangely, Richard felt a little nervous. The show was scheduled to begin at seven-thirty and the performers had been told to arrive at least two hours early. Richard had offered to drive Joanna to the town hall and she'd been sitting next to him in his car for the last ten minutes, gazing out the window and biting her lip. He wondered if she was suffering pre-performance jitters as well. He pulled up at traffic lights as they changed to orange.

'How are you feeling?' he enquired.

'Okay.' She shifted her gaze briefly but then resumed looking out the window.

'You look great.'

Male members of the hospital staff who were performing had been instructed to wear black trousers and a white shirt and, for the women, their uniform for the night was a long black skirt and white top.

Joanna looked gorgeous. She was wearing a silky culotte-style, ankle-length skirt and a sheer long-sleeved blouse over a lacy white camisole that was clearly visible through the almost transparent fabric of her top. Since they'd not had a full dress rehearsal, the outfit was new to Richard—and the whole package took his breath away. She looked so feminine and elegant and sensual all at the same time.

'Thanks.'

She ran her fingers through her hair, which was now a couple of centimetres long and growing back thicker and darker than ever. Although the elfin style suited her, Richard was looking forward to longer locks that he could run his own fingers through.

In fact, he was full of hope that they would formalise a reconciliation when he took Jo out to dinner the following night. He hoped she'd be more relaxed by then and that the coolness that had descended like a sudden winter chill when he'd picked her up would dissipate when the mood of excited anticipation changed once the concert was behind them.

'You still okay for tomorrow night?'

The way she was behaving towards him at the moment made him wonder if she might have changed her mind.

She smiled but it looked forced.

'Yes, I'm looking forward to it.'

By that time they'd arrived at the venue of the concert and parked in an area designated for performers in the public re-serve across the road.

Richard hoisted his saxophone out of the back, locked up the car and they headed towards the hall. In the foyer, they caught up with a group of chattering nurses from one of the general medical wards, which signalled the end of any chance of one-to-one conversation. Joanna seemed to disappear into the middle of the group and before Richard realised she was gone he was being corralled by Jodie Francis into the area on the stage designated for the band. With the twenty-voice female choir, the band was to stay on stage for the whole show. Individual performers would come and go and the poignant, happy-sad and sometimes funny video footage would be played in two blocks—one just before intermission and the other at the conclusion. Although he'd only seen parts of the film, Richard had been impressed. Lorraine and Steve had done an excellent job.

The next hour and a half dragged and, after two cups of tea, half a ham sandwich, a quick run through a number that had been included at the last minute and the interminable prattle of Jodie Francis, Richard was relieved when the call for silence was finally made. As the curtain gracefully rose, the silence was broken by a 'squeaky wheel' sound coming from the side of the stage.

'Daisy?'

A loud, clear voice, without an owner, added to the suspense.

'Daisy!' the voice boomed, as a clown zigzagged his way onto the stage on a rickety old tandem bicycle.

'Where are you, Daisy?'

A girl of about fourteen or fifteen, who Richard knew was a survivor of childhood leukaemia, heavily made up and wearing a Dorothy from *The Wizard of Oz* style dress sidled onto the stage.

That was the cue for the band to softly play the opening bars of 'Bicycle Built for Two'. The volume of the music gradually increased as the clown began to serenade the teenager and then the choir joined in for the chorus.

When the song finished the audience burst into rapturous applause and the mood was set for the rest of the evening— one of light-hearted, fun-filled family entertainment.

The next few hours flew by with a mix of music, song, laughs and film. From the audience response, one of the most popular segments was the video footage of the children in the hospital wards. The capacity crowd was rapt, from Karen's lively little group of toddlers, to a spectacular solo from Danny Sims, a segment of fragmentary 'knock-knock' jokes that Steve had somehow melded together perfectly and everything in between.

It was a brilliant performance from a cast of close to a hundred.

Just before the closing video segment, another song had been added to the programme that hadn't been rehearsed. It wasn't a melody that lent itself to sax playing so Richard had the luxury of sitting back and watching. He was curious to see who was to be the solo vocalist for the well-known John Lennon song.

He didn't have to wait very long.

Considerable ceremony was made of hauling an antique rocking chair onto the stage. A woman carrying a small child of about two or three walked, barefoot and draped in a lacy sunshine-yellow crocheted shawl, onto centre stage. She sat down and began to rock slowly, her total attention focused on the child.

A moment later the band began to play to the rhythm of the mesmerising movement and the woman began to sing.

The audience was totally silent as, in a pure, uplifting voice Joanna sang the simple, moving lullaby. It told about a father's love for his son; his impatience in wanting the boy to come of age; and his promise to guide the child through his life's journey, whatever happened.

He knew that Joanna was singing not only for the child sitting, enraptured, on her knee…but for him…and Sam, their *beautiful, beautiful boy.*

The words travelled like an arrow, straight to his heart,

and he was almost certain, as the melody softly faded, that the last words Joanna sang in what was close to a whisper were 'darling Sam'.

Richard waited for the band to finish, and the final video segment to begin before he quietly got up from his seat and slipped away, off the stage and out of the hall into the cool night air.

And he walked…and walked…and walked.

Twenty minutes later, in a dark, quiet street, he began to cry. Silent tears at first, then uncontrollable sobs.

For Sam.

For the loss of a child he couldn't bring back.

For the gift of his own life that he would have willingly traded for his son's.

For the love of a woman he couldn't bear to lose.

The sense of relief was incredible.

Joanna had been right.

She had shown him something that had eluded him for the past three years—how to grieve for Sam.

How to cry.

CHAPTER NINE

EXCITEMENT was a strange feeling to be having at the prospect of taking Joanna out on a date, but there was no other way to describe it. During Richard's time in the U.K. he'd dated half a dozen women, enjoyed the company of a couple enough to want to go out with them more than once but they'd never *excited* him. And he'd not had the faintest desire to take any of them home and get tangled up in *strings*.

With Joanna it was different. He wanted *strings*. Desperately. With his heart, body and soul. He knew, if they started over, it would be on different turf. They had both changed but not to the point where they'd lost the connection that had led to their marriage in the first place.

He wanted to make their evening something truly special. He wanted to reaffirm their marriage and suggest they try living together again. He was willing but it all depended on Joanna, and over the last two weeks she'd done her best to avoid him.

So he decided he'd surprise her in more ways than one and he hoped he'd have the time to put his plans into place.

First he showered and shaved. He changed into freshly cleaned and pressed navy-blue casual trousers and a crisp white shirt with the faintest navy stripe. He pocketed his tie. Even the smartest restaurants rarely insisted on ties these days but he didn't want to be caught short. As an afterthought he grabbed a jacket but he doubted he'd need it as it was an exceptionally warm evening.

Then he got in his car and drove to the nearby weekend markets, already bustling with early evening trade.

His business in the markets didn't take long. He chose roses—a dozen long-stemmed, sunshine-yellow buds—from the busy florist. His next port of call was the chocolatier where he selected a simple clear-topped rectangular box of an exquisite, hand-made combination of dark and light confections, tied with a yellow ribbon. Lastly he went to the jeweller to pick up the pendant he'd ordered a fortnight ago.

He smiled as he placed the small box in his pocket and gently laid the rest of his purchases on the back seat of his car. By that time it was a quarter to seven so he decided to while away a pleasant half-hour across the road at the recently restored Premier Hotel. He rarely spent time drinking in pubs but when he did he usually enjoyed the rowdy cheerfulness of the patrons and the interactions of the young people playing out the public mating rituals that seemed to change little over the years.

His sojourn in the popular front bar, including one tall glass of iced mineral water, served its purpose. He was feeling relaxed and primed with pleasant anticipation as he left the hotel, crossed the road and walked down the pavement towards the traffic lights not far from where he'd parked his car.

Before he was able to register the speed of the motorbike accelerating to beat the red light, it braked, swerved onto the footpath, narrowly missing a woman with a pram, waiting to cross, and then bulldozed into a shopfront—right where he stood.

The pain in his side was excruciating; the blow to his head transformed the scene to slow motion for what must only have been seconds before he blacked out.

* * *

Joanna had mixed feelings about her date with Richard. It was a big night for her and she had psyched herself up to tell him all—first that she was pregnant and, depending on how he reacted to that monumental piece of news, that she still loved him and was seriously prepared to try again. She knew if that happened there would be many hurdles but she felt strong enough to cope this time. Even if they lost the baby… She felt, with Richard's help, she now had the strength to survive.

She had plenty of time to get ready as she wanted to look her best. After a long, lingering shower, she towelled herself dry and automatically looked down at her belly. If her dates were right she'd be about two months pregnant, the baby growing inside her now fully formed and roughly the size of a broad bean. Approximately the same length as her two-centimetre-long hair.

She smiled and then grabbed her robe, walked through to the bedroom and stared at her face in the mirror. Grimacing at the pallor of her skin and the faint dark rings under her eyes, she opened her make-up drawer. Twenty minutes later she did a reappraisal and was happy with the result. It was amazing what a difference a soft beige foundation, some blusher and smear of deep crimson lipstick could do. She rarely wore eye make-up but completed the look with a light application of mascara.

Now the dress.

She slipped the shimmery black mini-dress over her head and stretched behind her to do up the zip. Glad of the kilo of weight she'd lost due to her unpredictable appetite, she smoothed the slightly flared skirt and adjusted her full breasts in what now seemed a skimpy and seductive bodice. The V of the neckline was too revealing and the straps too narrow. She hadn't known she was pregnant when she'd bought the dress and hadn't expected to be at least a bra size bigger.

But she didn't have time to change. Instead she fastened a

velvet choker around her neck and slipped a black lacy wrap around her shoulders

She glanced at her watch and noted, with alarm, she was running late. But so was Richard. It was twenty to eight already and he'd said they'd leave at seven-thirty. Not that she minded but it had been a long time since lunch and she was getting hungry.

Strange...

Where on earth was he?

Should she be worried?

No, of course not. He was a grown man, quite capable of looking after himself. But she couldn't help her concern. She was just deciding whether to be annoyed or apprehensive when the phone rang.

'That will be Richard,' she muttered as she padded into the living room in stockinged feet. 'He's been caught up with work.' *As inevitably happened to doctors on a public holiday weekend*, she added in her mind as she picked up the phone.

'Hello.'

There was a pause.

'Richard?' she said tentatively.

'Is that Joanna Raven?' It was a female voice she didn't recognise.

'Yes.'

'My name's Sue.'

'Sue?' The woman sounded as if Joanna should know who she was but she couldn't place her.

'Yes, Sue Tyler, RN in the emergency department of Perth General. I may have spoken to you on the phone. You work in Oncology at Lady Lawler, don't you?'

She vaguely remembered the woman but wondered why she would be ringing her at home. Maybe it was something to do with the reason Richard had been delayed. There was a strong link between the oncology departments of both hospitals. Childhood cancer survivors grew into adults and at some stage were transferred. Information from and consultation with their paediatric specialists was often important.

'I'm ringing about Dr Howell.'

Now it made sense. He *had* been caught up in some sort of emergency and he couldn't get away.

'What's happened?' she said, assuming she'd end up having a sandwich for dinner and spend the rest of the evening watching TV.

'He's been involved in an accident—'

'What? What did you say?' The implications of what the nurse said suddenly hit home. 'What happened? What sort of accident? Is he hurt?'

'He's only just come in by ambulance and the boss, James Headland, and the team are with him now in the resuscitation room.'

Only the most seriously injured went straight to the resuscitation suite. It meant he was... She didn't want to imagine how bad he was. She needed to find out for herself.

The nurse was still speaking, though, attempting to answer her questions.

'He has a fracture of his left femur and a head injury. That's all I can tell you so far. He was unconscious when he arrived but regained consciousness for a few minutes and was asking for you so that's why I'm ringing. He insisted he wanted you and nobody else.'

'Okay, Sue. Thanks, I'll be there in fifteen minutes.'

Joanna slipped on her work shoes, grabbed her keys and ran out the door to her car. Richard had been in a serious accident and he could be dying! My God, she thought. How could this happen? Why did all the good things in her life have to be snatched away from her? What had Richard done—kind, gentle, wonderful Richard—to deserve this?

But she mustn't jump to conclusions, or imagine the worst,

she reminded herself as she resisted the temptation to put the accelerator of her nippy little car to the floor.

He was being resuscitated!

She needed to stay calm and focused.

He had a broken leg and had bumped his head. He was probably being assessed in Resus to determine the extent of his injuries, to make sure he was stable before tests such as X-rays and scans were done to clarify how badly he was hurt. He was in good hands. He had the best doctors and nurses looking after him. He would get through this and she would be there to help him.

Worrying sick about him wasn't going to change the outcome. She needed to stay calm.

She parked in a drop-off-only bay near the entrance to the emergency department, knowing she would be longer than fifteen minutes but thinking that was the least of her problems at that moment.

She arrived at Reception in the busy casualty department, breathing hard, her heart thumping. Fortunately a message had been left that she could be shown straight in to the treatment areas. The first thing she noticed was that two resuscitation rooms were occupied and she knew she couldn't burst in on the important work being done. Then she saw a nurse coming towards her. She was smiling.

'Hi. You must be Joanna.'

'That's right. How's Richard?'

Joanna curtailed her impatience. She knew what it was like to work in a hospital. Protocols had to be adhered to, rules obeyed. No matter how much she wanted to demand to see Richard, to make sure he was alive, to tell him how much she loved him…

'He's okay. He's stable and is off for X-rays and a CT of his head any minute now.' The nurse grasped her hand and gave it a gentle squeeze.

'Is he awake?'

'Yes, though drowsy. He's got an impressive haematoma on his forehead, though.'

Joanna sighed with relief, although she still nursed a ball of tension that felt like a watermelon sitting in her stomach.

'Can I see him?'

'I'll just check with James. But there shouldn't be any problem with you sitting with him, at least until he goes off for scans.'

'Thank you,' she said as she was directed towards a seat.

She chose to stand and the next few minutes felt like an eternity.

Richard remembered the collision and the pain that had followed but nothing of the ambulance journey or his admission to the emergency department of the Perth General Hospital. When he regained consciousness—he knew he must have been unconscious as it was the only reasonable explanation for his memory lapse—the first thing he was aware of was the noise. It was a cacophony. Like being woken by a full symphony orchestra playing Beethoven's Fifth out of tune.

He opened his eyes briefly, but immediately closed them against the dazzle of an overhead light with the strength of a searchlight. He had a mask over his face so he decided not to even try to speak. In amongst at least half a dozen beeping sounds he heard an unfamiliar female voice so loud he wanted to cover his ears. But his hands felt bound, his arms heavy and he had a needle-like pain jabbing at his wrist.

What was all the fuss about? It sounded as if he was on the wrong side of a scenario being played out in a hospital TV soap.

'He's awake, James. Opened his eyes,' the woman shouted.

'BP stable, one ten over eighty,' someone else called out.

'Good, start the second bag of Haemaccel.'

A man, who smelled of coffee and mint, leaned close and again shouted. *Do they think I'm hard of hearing?* Richard wondered.

'Open your eyes, Richard.'

No please or thank you. An order barked in the voice of an army sergeant.

'Are you awake? Open your eyes.'

Richard had the feeling the man wasn't going to go away until he did his bidding, so he opened his eyes and said what he really wanted.

'Where's Joanna?'

The man with the coffee-mint breath loomed close. He wore green surgical scrubs and had the air of a man who was used to giving orders and having them obeyed without question. Richard assumed he was a doctor and someone fairly high in the pecking order. His fuddled mind was clearing a little.

'What did you say?'

'He said, "Where's Joanna?"'

At last, a voice soft with compassion. Unlike the others, she saw no need to shout. Someone he could talk to, knowing she would hear what he needed to say.

'Who is Joanna?' she said. 'Is she your wife?'

Someone had turned the light away from his face and he could see the owner of the kind voice. She also wore green scrubs but he couldn't tell if she was a doctor or a nurse. He squinted at her name badge.

'Sue?'

'That's right. I'm a nurse. You had an accident outside the markets and you're in the emergency department of the General. Do you remember anything?'

The noise had gradually abated and there were only two people that he could see in the room now. The loud doctor had left him in the care of the quiet nurse but he expected him to be back.

'Yes.' He remembered buying roses and chocolates, having a quiet drink at the pub to pass some time. He'd had a date with Joanna and it had all gone wrong.

'Is Joanna your wife?'

'Yes,' he said without hesitation. 'But we're separated and she uses her maiden name, Raven. She's a nurse.'

The effort of speaking only a couple of sentences was taking its toll but he wasn't going to give up until someone contacted Joanna.

'I need to see her.'

'How can we contact her?'

'Her home number is in my mobile.'

He heard the nurse rummage somewhere below his feet and then he saw she had the standard blue plastic bag containing his possessions.

'You had your phone with you?'

'Yes.'

'Ah. Here it is. Looks like it came off better in the accident than you. Not a scratch on it. Is it okay if I look for her number?'

'Yes.'

'And tell her what we know so far.'

'And…er.' He was about to tell this person, Sue, to apologise on his behalf. To tell Joanna he was sorry for making such a mess of something that could have been wonderful. The acuteness of his pain and the fuzz around the edges of his mind were enough to make him realise there was morphine dripping into one of the IV lines in his arm. He also realised the only person who could explain those things to Joanna was him.

'Tell her I need to see her.'

'I will.'

Just then the doctor returned and he heard the sound of his voice, now quiet, muttering to Sue but not loud enough for him to hear, and he suddenly felt annoyed. His emotions seemed to be cascading out of control and he knew that some of what came into his head and threatened to come out of his mouth was out of character but he felt he had to tell Dr Coffee-mint there was no need to whisper.

Somehow his hand found his mouth and he pulled down the mask.

'I'd like to hear what you're saying about me. I'm a doctor and want the facts.'

The man smiled.

'I see you're getting better, then. Good to have you back, Dr Howell.' He moved nearer to the head of the bed and stood with both hands on the side rails. 'I'll need to examine you again now you can tell me where it hurts, though the analgesia should be working well by now. Where's your pain?'

'My left thigh, left ankle and left shoulder.' He could see the splint and presumed he had a fractured femur. 'I've got a generalised dull headache and an ache across my lower back.'

'No gut pains?'

'Just a bit of nausea.'

'Chest pains?'

'Not really.'

Unless you consider a whole body ache to include the sum of all the parts.

'Breathing problems?'

'No.' Richard tolerated the mask being put back over his mouth but couldn't help asking, 'How am I doing, then?'

'Remarkably well, considering…' The man's expression turned serious as his voice trailed off and then he added, 'In fact, you're a very lucky man. But you won't be doing any doctoring for a while.'

He went on to explain he had an obvious leg fracture, the nature of which needed to be confirmed by X-rays, but he was ninety per cent certain he would need surgery to fix it. He would also order X-rays of several other areas of his skeleton they suspected might be damaged. A CT scan of his head would be performed and after that he would be transferred to a general acute bed in the ED and await assessment by the orthopaedic surgeon and the neurologist.

The realisation of how close to being killed he had come suddenly struck Richard and he spoke quietly as the doctor was about to leave.

'Thank you for what you've done.'

'My pleasure.' The man turned and extended his hand. 'I'm James Headland. I don't think we've met, before tonight, that is. I'm one of the ED consultants.' As they shook hands he added, 'I've heard of the good work you do and I reckon your job's a lot harder than mine.'

At that moment Sue breezed in.

'You'll be off to Radiology in the next ten minutes or so.' Then she grinned. 'And your wife is here.'

'Richard?'

Joanna had a full thirty seconds standing behind the nurse before Richard noticed she was there. During that time a dozen different emotions battled with each other for her attention.

Her first and most overwhelming feeling was fear. Lying battered and bruised on the ED trolley and hooked up to an alarming number of monitors as well as two IVs, Richard was almost unrecognisable. He peered through swollen eyelids and appeared to be battling to remove the oxygen mask the nurse insisted on repositioning.

His left leg was immobilised in an air splint and a blood-soaked dressing covered his upper arm.

'Richard,' she said, a little louder. She suppressed an almost irresistible urge to rush to him and embrace him, kiss his swollen face and offer comfort with whatever resources she could muster. But he would be hurting and she didn't want to make his pain any worse.

'Joanna, you came.' He suddenly noticed her and his initial attempt to smile turned into a grimace.

A mixture of relief and overpowering, all-consuming, gut-wrenching love took over her fear—he was alive and at least trying, though not too successfully, for cheerfulness.

'I'll just replace this dressing,' Sue said as she donned gloves and replaced the sodden gauze and anchored it with a bandage. 'How is your pain?'

'Bearable,' Richard said with a frustrated edge to his voice.

'Out of ten?'

'Seven, maybe six.' His voice croaked and he frowned as he cleared his throat. Joanna's heart went out to him. She could imagine him playing down his injuries for her benefit and by the tortured look on his face it was probably pain keeping him from drifting into a morphine-induced sleep.

'Improving, then?'

'A little.'

'Okay. As long as your BP's stable and normal Dr Headland's ordered a bolus of painkiller before you have your X-rays. I'll just check your blood pressure and then leave you two until the orderly comes.'

There was a brief moment of awkwardness when the nurse left but it didn't take long before silent tears began running down Joanna's cheeks and she leaned forward and kissed Richard on his bruised forehead.

'I'm sorry...' he whispered.

Joanna pulled herself away and reached for his hand.

'No, how can you say that? You're apologising?'

'I wanted…' He managed to pull off the mask and his words were husky with emotion. 'I wanted to tell you…' He hesitated as if he was choosing his words carefully. 'I wanted tonight to be special.' He paused again and took a moment to look at her as well as catch his breath. 'Look at you. You're the most beautiful woman…'

He closed his eyes and Joanna tried to wipe away her tears but she couldn't stop them. Richard was lying in the resuscitation room, his body broken and no doubt facing a long and difficult road back to health, and all he was thinking about was her.

'Shush.' She laid a finger gently on his lips and was surprised at the coolness of his skin. 'You don't need to tell me this now. Save your energy.'

'But I need to tell you. Before I go… If I have surgery…'

She suddenly realised he was thinking of the possibility of not surviving and she couldn't bear it. She stopped crying and took a deep breath.

'Don't even think about it, Richard Howell. Not now or ever.'

He frowned and said quietly, 'I don't understand.'

'I've fallen in love with you all over again,' she whispered. 'And I'm not going to let you have the slightest thought that you might leave me.'

The tears began again and this time a single drop of moisture escaped from Richard's eye but he was smiling a devilishly crooked smile.

'That's just what I was trying to tell you.'

The door swung open and James Headland stood in the doorway with an orderly behind him.

'How are you now?' he asked as he grabbed the chart and nodded his approval.

'Much better.'

He sent a glance in Joanna's direction and she knew Richard would come through this. He was bracing himself for whatever it took and she was going to be there with him—all the way.

Joanna accompanied Richard to the X-ray department and then sat with him while he waited for the orthopaedic surgeon's assessment. She shared the news that he needed the fracture of his femur fixed with an intramedullary nail—the sooner the better—and then anxiously waited four long hours while he was in surgery. The time dragged and she was overwhelmed with the news, at just after two in the morning, that the operation had been a success.

'When can I see him?' she asked the surgeon when he emerged from the operating rooms looking as weary as Joanna felt.

'It will probably be another hour before he's ready for transfer to Intensive Care—'

'ICU! Is there something wrong?'

The surgeon must have read the look on her face as alarm. He touched her arm.

'No, nothing's wrong. Everything went smoothly in Theatre. He's had a head injury, though, and lost a lot of blood. It's just a precaution to watch him overnight, give him another unit of blood, make sure he's stable before transferring him to the orthopaedic ward.'

Joanna still couldn't relax and wasn't going to leave until she saw him, even if it meant staying at the hospital all night.

'So when can I see him?' she repeated. 'I need to know—'

The surgeon sighed. 'You're his wife, are you?'

'Yes.' Joanna was surprised how easy it was to slip into that role.

'And a paediatric nurse?'

'That's right.' She tried her hardest not to sound impatient.

'If you put on a gown, mask and cap, you can pop into Recovery. It's unlikely he'll be awake as he's on a fairly hefty dose of morphine. In fact, the best thing you can do after you see him would be to go home and get some rest. He should be well enough to have a visitor late this afternoon.'

What he was saying made sense and she was grateful for the time the doctor had spent with her and the concession he'd made in allowing her to go into the recovery ward.

'Thank you.' She held out her hand and he shook it briefly.

'The change rooms are down there.' He nodded in the direction of the operating theatres just before he strode away. Then he stopped and turned, smiling. 'He's lucky to have you and I'm as certain as I can be that he'll recover.'

Joanna knew that nothing was certain in medicine but she accepted the reassurance and told herself something she often said to the distraught relatives of her own patients—that wasting energy on worrying achieved nothing. But she only half convinced herself and her anxiety escalated when, after quickly changing, she arrived in the recovery room.

'You must be Mrs Howell?' The nurse looked up briefly before glancing at the bag dripping blood into a vein in Richard's arm and writing something on his chart.

'Yes.' The word came out as a whisper. She felt herself flushing.

From what she could see of Richard, he looked deathly pale and seemed to be hooked up to even more monitoring equipment than in the emergency department. The nurse beckoned her to come closer.

'The anaesthetist has just taken his endotracheal tube out. He's breathing well on his own and he even opened his eyes. He'll probably be on the move within the next half-hour. He's doing really well.'

Joanna sidled up to the trolley and tucked her fingers into the palm of one of his hands. He showed no sign of wakefulness at first but then slowly opened his eyes. His face, still swollen, had darkened with more bruising over the hours he had been in surgery.

'Richard?'

His eyes slowly closed, as if it had been a great effort to open them but, under the mask, she could tell he was trying to say something.

'Don't try and talk. I just needed to see you.' She didn't add that she'd wanted to make sure he was still alive, and that she was scared and confused, balanced on the edge of a bunch of emotions she hadn't fully come to grips with. Her grief at the prospect of losing him had been acute and overwhelming.

She leaned over and kissed his cheek and in a husky whisper Joanna could barely understand he said, 'I love you, Jo. I always have and I always will.' His eyes opened again and were full of passion. 'So much that it hurts more than...' He squeezed her hand and then, before she had a chance to answer, he drifted off into a deep sleep. She could barely hold back the tears.

It must have been scarcely a minute or two that Joanna stood staring at the battered figure of the man she loved, but it seemed like an age. There was so much she wanted to tell him, so many words that had been left unsaid.

She turned as she felt a gentle hand on her shoulder.

'Mr Nichols said you could only have five minutes. I'm sorry...'

'I know. Thank you.'

She leaned close and kissed Richard again, whispering the same words he'd made such an effort to say to her a minute ago but knowing he wouldn't hear her.

'I'm sorry, but...' The nurse smiled.

'Yes, I know I must go.'

Joanna released Richard's hand and walked out of the

ward, suddenly overcome with tiredness. She needed to go home to try and get some sleep.

Richard groaned.

The dull pain in his leg was unremitting but bearable, as long as he didn't move.

'What the hell...?' he muttered, then opened his eyes, glanced around him, and remembered.

He was in hospital. There'd been an accident—a nasty one—and he'd had an operation. He remembered a dream, so vivid it could almost have been real. He'd seen Joanna. His beautiful, caring, Joanna—and he'd told her he loved her.

The door of his room slowly opened and he was surprised at the ferocity of his desire for it to be her.

'Dr Howell, you're finally awake.'

Disappointment.

The middle-aged nurse bore no resemblance to his darling Jo.

Very perceptive of you to notice, he felt like saying, but simply nodded instead.

'Good.' She wheeled in the hardware required to do his obs. 'How is the pain?'

He flinched as she looked as if she was about to prod his heavily bandaged leg but instead pinched his big toe.

'Ouch.' He uttered the protest out of surprise more than genuine pain but the ache in his leg seemed to go up a notch. The nurse raised her black, pencilled eyebrows but thankfully didn't comment.

'Seven out of ten,' he finally said with a frown. He thought he had a reasonably high tolerance to pain, but he hadn't broken the biggest long-bone in his body before.

'I'll give you a bolus of morphine, then, and now you're awake I'll organise PCA. I assume you know what that means.'

'Yes.' He didn't have the energy to verify he was familiar with the system where he could give his own medication, the so-called *patient-controlled analgesia.*

The nurse checked his BP, temperature and oxygen saturation as well as his urine output. She jotted a note on his chart and told him she would be back in five or ten minutes with the morphine.

'And you have a visitor.'

It was then he noticed Joanna hovering in the doorway with a broad grin on her face. It lasted only a moment and then her brow furrowed in an expression he'd seen many times.

Something was wrong. What had upset her? He wasn't fooled by the smile and he was pretty sure his mind was clear, despite the cocktail of medications coursing through his veins.

'Come in, Joanna.' He went to stretch out his arms to give her a hug but got caught up in a tangle of tubes and wires. Before he had time to apologise she was at his bedside, her hands resting lightly on his shoulders, her soft, warm lips on his cheek. God, her touch was more therapeutic than any drugs.

'What time is it? I hope you haven't been here all night.' He glanced at the window, covered with Venetian blinds open just enough to see slivers of sky tinged with the orange-gold of a rising sun… Or was it setting?

'I left about half past two this morning, after your op, and when I phoned at lunchtime they said you were still out of it.' She ran gentle fingers over the back of his hand that wasn't connected to an IV tube. Her touch felt so good. 'It's nearly seven o'clock.'

He paused for a moment, taking in what she'd said. He'd lost an entire day.

'At night? And it's Monday?'

'That's right.'

She withdrew her hand and pulled a chair close to the bed but he still had the impression something was wrong. Had the operation not gone as well as he had been led to believe? Had he done something to upset her? He couldn't imagine what. He'd been unconscious for most of the day. Perhaps something had happened that had nothing to do with him. The thoughts began to spin in his head and he closed his eyes and took a couple of steadying breaths.

'There's something wrong, Jo. I can tell you're upset. I know you must have been to hell and back over the last twenty-four hours but—'

'There's nothing wrong.' She smiled with a return of the old warmth that he knew so well. 'But, yes, it's been a strain. I'm not the one with a metal spike in my leg, though, and a face that bears an uncanny resemblance to a half-inflated soccer ball.'

He laughed. And his awareness of the pain in his leg increased, but he felt a little better.

At that moment the nurse came in with his analgesia. She glanced at Joanna, who stood and dragged the chair a little away from the bed to give the nurse access to the arm with the drip.

'Are you happy to stay while I set up the PCA?'

'If it's okay with you.'

'No problem.'

Richard felt the effect of the bolus of medication almost immediately. The throbbing in his leg eased and a swooning light-headedness made the room spin. He closed his eyes and that was the last thing he clearly remembered until he felt a gentle squeeze of his hand.

'I'm going now.'

He saw Joanna through a fuddled haze.

'So soon? You've only just arrived.'

'You've been asleep for...' she looked at her watch '...five hours. It's past midnight and I have to work tomorrow. I have an early. I'll come in and see you after work.' She grinned. 'And Mr Nichols made a brief appearance and said you're doing great.'

'Midnight? I'm sorry… Of course you must go… Come here.'

He kissed her hand, drew her close then kissed her lips.

He wanted to reaffirm that he loved her but she pulled away, patted his hand and left the room before he could even say goodbye.

His earlier worries came rolling back. Something was definitely wrong. His heart did an uncomfortable somersault and then fell with a heavy thud and came to rest in the pit of his stomach.

She'd stopped loving him. And he was somehow to blame.

Joanna couldn't tell him. It was too soon after his operation and it wasn't fair to add her life-changing news when he'd been through what she assumed was one of the biggest traumas of his life.

She decided she'd leave it at least a few days, until he was over the worst of his post-operative pain. She'd know when the time was right. Or at least that's what she kept telling herself, over and over.

She'd know when the time was right.

It was the fourth post-operative day and, apart from a nagging pain in his left thigh when the physio cajoled him into his daily exercises, Richard was feeling nearly normal. He had started eating and actually enjoying the hospital food. One of the IV lines and his urinary catheter had been removed the previous day and the frequency of his morphine injections was decreasing and being replaced by tablets.

What had been his prime motivation to make as speedy

a recovery as he could was Joanna. She'd visited every day and they'd managed to fill in an hour or two chatting about the goings-on in Matilda Ward—how Alan Price had apparently welcomed a break in his retirement to return to work, Karen's new boyfriend, the death of Barbara's elderly father from a heart attack, and a dozen other snippets of inconsequential gossip.

Joanna seemed to have developed an uncanny knack for avoiding discussion of anything more personal than work, though.

So he was going to talk to her today. To explain that the dinner that had never happened was all part of a surprise that he hoped she'd be pleased with.

She was due any minute and he felt strangely nervous.

Half an hour later she arrived, looking absolutely gorgeous in a gauzy, floaty mini-dress that wasn't sheer enough to be transparent but it certainly drew attention to Joanna's feminine attributes.

'You look fabulous,' he said with a grin. 'I love the dress.'

Her cheeks flushed. 'It's new. They had a fifty per cent off sale at Jenny Lee's.'

'It really suits you.'

'Thanks.'

Small talk was all they'd managed over the last couple of days and Richard wondered if a serious talk would clear the air and at least restore their relationship to where it had been before the accident. Perhaps the drama of his injuries had swept them up in the *idea* that they loved each other but now she was having second thoughts.

Second thoughts? Was it possible?

He knew he still loved Joanna and he'd believed what she'd said on the night of the accident—that she loved him. But now he was beginning to have doubts of his own and was confused about whether the feeling was still reciprocated. Or perhaps she had told him in the heat of the moment.

Joanna rummaged in her bag and brought out a packet of photographs.

'Lynne organised these. She said it might help you realise how much the staff and the kids all miss you.' Her smile was one of genuine affection, most likely for her young charges whose smiles lit each snapshot.

'They're fabulous. Can you make sure you thank Lynne for me?'

'Perhaps you can tell her yourself. She said she'd come and visit on the weekend.'

'With her camera, no doubt.'

'Of course.'

The conversation dried up and Joanna began fiddling with the photos. He took them from her, put them away in the drawer of his bedside cabinet and grasped both her hands in his.

'We need to talk.'

'Yes,' she said in a quiet voice. Then she presented him with a heart-melting look and added, 'About our future.'

'That's right.'

Richard was about to continue: to try and explain how much he wanted the marriage to work again; to tell her he couldn't imagine spending the rest of his life with anyone else.

But she spoke first in a trembling voice so quiet he didn't quite hear what she said. At first he thought she'd said, 'I'm pregnant,' but he knew that was impossible.

'Pardon?'

She cleared her throat and reached for his hand.

'I'm pregnant.'

There was no mistaking the words this time. He beamed,

not quite believing that she was telling the truth but thinking there was no reason for her to lie.

'Pregnant?'

She nodded, a smile spreading across her face.

'But—'

'We didn't believe it was possible, but we've been given another chance, Richard, another chance to bring a child into this world.' She took a deep breath and the tears began to trickle down her cheeks. 'And I'm scared to death.'

He spread his arms and reached out to her and she dissolved in his embrace.

'We're in this together, my darling Jo,' he managed to say, before tears started streaming down his own face.

They were tears of happiness.

It appeared all his dreams were coming true.

CHAPTER TEN

THE next month turned out to be an ordeal for both Richard and Joanna. Despite the pain and frustration of what seemed to be a never-ending struggle to get Richard back on his feet, an unfailing light shone bright to keep them both moving forward with hope and optimism.

That light was their love for each other, which was fuelled by the knowledge of the new life they had created. That love survived and sustained them through those awful early days of tests and surgery and not knowing.

Fortunately Richard's only broken bone had been his femur, which had apparently taken the full impact of the motorbike and snapped in two. Its repair had involved surgery to insert an intramedullary nail to hold the broken ends in place over the many months it would take the fracture to heal. Joanna still cringed at the thought of a massive nail being hammered through the top of the femur at the hip down the hollow part inside the main bone of the leg.

His other injuries had been relatively minor—concussion with no sign of long-term brain injury, a dislocated shoulder, a badly bruised ankle and various cuts, abrasions and bruises.

'I'm beginning to hate the physio sessions,' he said on the Monday of the third week when Joanna called to see him at the rehabilitation hospital. He'd been transferred from Perth General the previous week, keen to at least learn the basics of day-to-day living so he could be discharged. He sat on a chair next to his bed. It was the first day she had seen him dressed in day clothes, the clothes he had insisted she bring when he had been moved. He looked even more handsome than usual.

She leaned across and kissed him, at first a light touch of her lips on his but he captured her face in his warm, strong hands and kissed her long and thoroughly until she had to pull away to catch her breath.

She laughed.

'You're feeling better, then?' she said.

'When can you take me away from all this, my wonderful fairy godmother?'

'You know they say doctors make the worst patients. Have you forgotten already what it's like, dealing with those stubborn souls who think they know best and don't do what they're told?'

He looked wistful for a moment.

'No, of course I haven't. That's why I want to get out of here. As soon as I can manage getting around on my own for longer than the regulation half-hour in this place, I should be able to at least touch base with work.'

Joanna chose to ignore his comment. She realised it would be a while before Richard was strutting the boards of Matilda Ward again but she had no doubt he would.

'You've had two days of rehab and you think you're ready to go back to work?'

He grinned sheepishly.

'No, not really.'

'Good, you're not as pig-headed as you pretend to be. And Alan Price is quite happy to interrupt his retirement. He actually said he'd become bored with golf.'

'Not too happy, I hope,' he said with a grin, and then added,

'Patience is something I've had to learn quickly here to stop me going insane.'

'Mmm.'

They sat in comfortable silence for a minute or two, holding hands. Richard had a single room on the second floor, overlooking an expanse of garden crisscrossed by several meandering, wheelchair-friendly paths. Joanna was impatient for the day they could walk together through the gardens and hoped it wouldn't be too long.

Richard had been told by his surgeon that early intervention following surgery focused on immediate weight bearing and then progression to strengthening exercises. She'd been amazed at his progress and suspected in those early post-op days he'd made a heroic effort to work though his pain without complaint.

Richard and Joanna decided to reaffirm their vows in the second week of spring to allow Richard's bones to heal and to give them plenty of time to make sure the day was as wonderful as it could possibly be. Joanna would be nearly six months pregnant by then. They decided on a small morning ceremony in one of their favourite places followed by a lunch for a group of close family and friends in the recently renovated and landscaped garden of their spacious new home. On a Saturday in mid-September it dawned an ideal day for a wonderful wedding and by mid-morning the small group of guests had assembled.

Joanna held a bouquet of yellow, perfectly formed, sweet-smelling rosebuds, which complemented the delicately feminine, cream silk dress that was softly gathered below the bust to accommodate her now very obvious pregnancy. Richard looked elegant and sexy and gorgeous all at the same time in a tailored black suit, the palest lemon-yellow shirt and a silver-grey tie.

The second-time bride hesitated as she reached up to tame a feral lock escaped from her dark glossy cap, still a long way from reaching her pale, bare shoulders. His smile reached out to her like the first sunlit rays of a delicate spring dawn and her husband made her feel so special in an amazing way she'd always dreamed he would…again.

They stood at the makeshift altar in the secret courtyard garden of Lady Lawler Children's Hospital amongst a crowd of beaming children. Some were on crutches; others were in wheelchairs hooked up to IVs and portable oxygen cylinders; many were bald and had the round faces of chemotherapy—but every single child was brimming over with happiness for the couple about to endorse their love and commitment.

Richard and Joanna recited their vows of love and caring to an audience hushed with anticipation, and then the clear, sweet voice of a boy soprano rang out in the crisp air of a perfect spring day. Danny Sims sang 'The Rose'.

Then a tiny girl in a long white dress toddled forward and presented the bride with a small posy of sweet-smelling freesias to add to her bouquet.

'From all us kids,' she said grandly.

Joanna bent forward and kissed the child's cheek.

'Thank you, Taylor,' Joanna whispered a moment before the little girl ran back to the protective arms of her smiling mother.

Richard squeezed his wife's hand.

'And I'd like to thank everyone here today for sharing our happiness. Though I'm afraid we can't put it off any longer: what you've all been waiting for; what started this whole thing with Joanna and I.'

The guests chuckled and then began to clap as Jessie and Cassie brought out a chair, Karen following close behind carrying a small case and what looked like a Spiderman cape slung across her arm.

Lynne and Barbara came next with sombre expressions on their faces.

With the theatrics of a circus ringmaster, Lynne led Richard to the chair. He sat down and Karen draped him in the cape while the noise of the clapping gradually increased to a crescendo.

Barbara raised her hands.

'Quiet, everyone.'

She beckoned Joanna to come across and handed her a set of battery-operated shears.

'Since Dr Howell…er…your husband is making this sacrifice for you and for all of us too, would you like to perform the first cut?'

Joanna laughed. 'No, I think I'll let you do the honours,' she said, as she bent to kiss her apprehensive husband.

'Are you sure you want to do this?' she added.

'Definitely. I've never been surer of anything in my entire life.'

And as the first locks began to fall Danny again began to sing…the opening verse of 'Wind Beneath My Wings'.

* * * * *

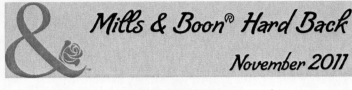

Mills & Boon® Hard Back

November 2011

ROMANCE

The Power of Vasilii	Penny Jordan
The Real Rio D'Aquila	Sandra Marton
A Shameful Consequence	Carol Marinelli
A Dangerous Infatuation	Chantelle Shaw
Kholodov's Last Mistress	Kate Hewitt
His Christmas Acquisition	Cathy Williams
The Argentine's Price	Maisey Yates
Captive but Forbidden	Lynn Raye Harris
On the First Night of Christmas...	Heidi Rice
The Power and the Glory	Kimberly Lang
How a Cowboy Stole Her Heart	Donna Alward
Tall, Dark, Texas Ranger	Patricia Thayer
The Secretary's Secret	Michelle Douglas
Rodeo Daddy	Soraya Lane
The Boy is Back in Town	Nina Harrington
Confessions of a Girl-Next-Door	Jackie Braun
Mistletoe, Midwife...Miracle Baby	Anne Fraser
Dynamite Doc or Christmas Dad?	Marion Lennox

HISTORICAL

The Lady Confesses	Carole Mortimer
The Dangerous Lord Darrington	Sarah Mallory
The Unconventional Maiden	June Francis
Her Battle-Scarred Knight	Meriel Fuller

MEDICAL ROMANCE™

The Child Who Rescued Christmas	Jessica Matthews
Firefighter With A Frozen Heart	Dianne Drake
How to Save a Marriage in a Million	Leonie Knight
Swallowbrook's Winter Bride	Abigail Gordon

GEN STD HB

ROMANCE

HISTORICAL

MEDICAL ROMANCE™

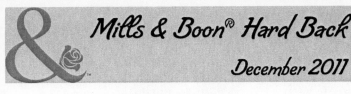

ROMANCE

Jewel in His Crown	Lynne Graham
The Man Every Woman Wants	Miranda Lee
Once a Ferrara Wife...	Sarah Morgan
Not Fit for a King?	Jane Porter
In Bed with a Stranger	India Grey
In a Storm of Scandal	Kim Lawrence
The Call of the Desert	Abby Green
Playing His Dangerous Game	Tina Duncan
How to Win the Dating War	Aimee Carson
Interview with the Daredevil	Nicola Marsh
Snowbound with Her Hero	Rebecca Winters
The Playboy's Gift	Teresa Carpenter
The Tycoon Who Healed Her Heart	Melissa James
Firefighter Under the Mistletoe	Melissa McClone
Flirting with Italian	Liz Fielding
The Inconvenient Laws of Attraction	Trish Wylie
The Night Before Christmas	Alison Roberts
Once a Good Girl...	Wendy S. Marcus

HISTORICAL

The Disappearing Duchess	Anne Herries
Improper Miss Darling	Gail Whitiker
Beauty and the Scarred Hero	Emily May
Butterfly Swords	Jeannie Lin

MEDICAL ROMANCE™

New Doc in Town	Meredith Webber
Orphan Under the Christmas Tree	Meredith Webber
Surgeon in a Wedding Dress	Sue MacKay
The Boy Who Made Them Love Again	Scarlet Wilson

Mills & Boon® Large Print

December 2011

ROMANCE

HISTORICAL

MEDICAL ROMANCE™